FAVOURITE

Māori

LEGENDS

LiBrO
INTERNATIONAL

Published by Libro International, an imprint of Oratia Media Ltd, 783 West Coast Road,
Oratia, Auckland 0604, New Zealand (www.librointernational.com).

ISBN 978-1-877514-56-2
Ebook ISBN 978-1-877514-58-6

Project editor: Carolyn Lagahetau
Designer: Cheryl Rowe, Macarn Design

First published 1965 by A.H. & A.W. Reed
This edition 2013 by Libro International

Printed in China

Contents

Foreword (1965)

For hundreds of years these stories have been told to Māori children and adults in the house of amusement at nights, or on the marae, by the storytellers and learned men of the tribes. They would not all be known to a single iwi or hapū (tribe or subtribe), for they come from every part of the islands of New Zealand, which were known to the Māori as Aotearoa.

We owe a great deal to the kaumātua, the learned elders, and to early students of Māori lore, for collecting these tales before they were forgotten by later generations. Amongst the notable collectors we may number J. Herries Beattie, Elsdon Best, Rev. William Colenso, James Cowan, A.A. Grace, Sir George Grey, Hare Hongi, J.H. Mitchell, Col. C.B. Porter, Edward Shortland, Rev. Richard Taylor, John White, C.A. Wilson and Rev. J.F.H. Wohlers, who recorded stories at first hand.

The title of the book may need a word of explanation. The more popular Māori legends will be found in *Myths and Legends of Maoriland*, while shorter legendary tales appear in *Maori Fables and Legendary Tales*, both by A.W. Reed. *Treasury of Maori Folklore* by the same compiler contains a vast collection of legends, folktales, and myths. The present compilation is drawn directly from this source. As the more comprehensive work has a limited circulation amongst students of Māori lore, *Favourite Maori Legends* reaches a wider circle of readers.

The legends were famous in their day. Over the years they have to a large extent been forgotten, but they should not be lost to the present and future people of Aotearoa. As we become more conscious of the contribution that Māori culture should make to our common heritage, we believe that they will again become favourite legends.

A.W. Reed
Wellington, 1965

Introduction

The stories in the original 1965 edition of this volume are derived from A.W. Reed's classic *Treasury of Maori Folklore* (1963). As a child growing up I remember this volume, with its distinctive orange-streaked-with-black dust jacket, sitting on our family's bookshelf alongside biographies of All Blacks and pictorial books featuring New Zealand landscapes — many also published by A.H. & A.W. Reed.

Of course, as a child I was daunted by the sheer scale of the *Treasury* and did not appreciate the prodigious feat of research and retelling that that volume represented. In it, A.W. Reed put his unique spin on material compiled from sources such as the *Journal of the Polynesian Society* and the *Transactions of the New Zealand Institute*, as well as classic tribal histories such as *Takitimu* by J.H. Mitchell and *Tainui* by L.G. Kelly.

The *Treasury of Maori Folklore* had long been out of print when in 2003 I was asked by Reed Publishing to produce a revised edition, which was published as the *Reed Book of Māori Mythology* in 2004. Reworking that volume was both enjoyable and rewarding, immersed as I was in Māori mythology and the traditional stories of the tūpuna. In creating the new edition I updated the context and interpretation of the stories and added back, where possible, the Māori text of waiata, karakia and whakataukī, corrected various errors that had crept in and added information about Reed's sources where I could.

In turn the *Reed Book of Māori Mythology* became the source for a further two books — *Taniwha, Giants and Supernatural Creatures* and *Earth, Ocean, Sky* — published by Penguin in 2008 under the Raupō imprint.

So I knew what I was in for when I was approached by Peter Dowling, former Publishing Manager of Reed Publishing, to revise *Favourite Māori Legends*. In doing this work it has always been reassuring to have the support of Ray Richards, who worked closely with A.W. Reed for many years. Ray has continued to safeguard Reed's literary legacy since his death in 1979.

While this current volume largely follows the original A.W. Reed text, I have removed unnecessary archaisms and made corrections to some details such as names and places, as well as following orthographic conventions for modern Māori. My hope is that I have not diminished the value of the narratives as stories, for A.W. Reed had undoubted gifts in storytelling and making traditional narratives widely accessible to a popular audience.

Will the stories presented here conflict in some details with other versions that are out there in written form and in people's memories? Of course they will. There is no 'correct version' of any of these stories. Each iwi, and in some cases hapū within an iwi, will have their own version. Indeed, some of the stories are of such antiquity that versions are preserved in the islands of Polynesia from where the ancestors came — in other words, some of the stories have survived for close to a thousand years through telling, listening, remembering and retelling.

Indeed, telling stories and listening to them was perhaps the most popular leisure activity in traditional Māori society. The fall of night signalled the end of the day's labours and ushered in communal leisure time. In particular, the inclement weather and long dark evenings of winter gave ample opportunity for storytelling. Listeners would be seated in a dark whare, dimly lit by flickering fires within pits and by torches made from bundles of maire wood. They would have been gripped by tales of taniwha and patupaiarehe, simultaneously covering their ears yet straining to hear each new, gruesome detail.

Pakiwaitara and pūrākau are general terms for stories and traditions. Kōrero takurua (winter-time stories) and kōrero ahiahi (stories told by the fire) are less reliable kinds of stories, more in the nature of jokes, yarns and anecdotes. As the names suggest, they were embroidered with the primary aim of entertainment.

Beyond entertainment, storytelling was an important means of transmitting history, whakapapa and other knowledge. Early missionaries were staggered at the ability of Māori to memorise and retain information, which was due to this oral tradition.

I hope you can accompany me in enjoying the stories within this volume and the window they give on to te ao tawhito, the traditional Māori world.

Mauri ora,

Ross Calman
Karori, Wellington
April 2013

THE LAND OF SPIRITS

Cape Rēinga is the extreme north-west point of the North Island of New Zealand. On the rocky promontory grew an ancient pōhutukawa tree, the roots or branches of which provided a ladder for the spirits to descend through the swirling waters to the fabulous land below.

Towards this departing place came a never-ending procession of the spirits of the dead. The Far North seems to be crowded with the ghostly, hurrying footsteps of the souls of people. There are weird stories that tell of onlookers seeing parties of travellers in the distance, making their way northwards. The travellers would disappear as the onlookers drew near, then reappear behind those watching.

The northern tribes heard the rustle and movement of countless unseen forms after a battle, when the warriors who had been slain made their final rendezvous in the world of light. It was said that chiefs could be distinguished from slaves, for the rangatira always passed to one side of a pātaka (food store), while the slaves walked underneath. These were living beliefs. In the northern pā the doors of kūmara pits faced north, with their backs to the passing wairua lest they enter and make the contents tapu.

At the edge of the long, windswept beaches and the hills, the gales sometimes tied the flax leaves in knots, but those who lived there knew that it was the work of the wairua, who had a longing for the land that gave them birth and sustained them. Leaves of nīkau, tree fern or bracken were left by those who had come from the inland parts, dune grass or seaweed by coast-dwellers.

The hill of Te Ārai, about halfway along Te Oneroa-a-Tōhē (Ninety Mile Beach), was a favourite place to deposit the leaf-tokens. Another hill provided a resting place for the spirits. This was Taumataihaumū, where the wairua paused in their journey and looked back over the land they had traversed. Here they wept and cut themselves with flakes of obsidian, and wove kōpare (mourning wreathes) from leaves.

At the hills named Waihokimai and Waiotioti they mourned and lacerated themselves, stripped off their clothes (which were made of the leaves of whārangi, mākuku and horopito), turned their backs on the familiar scene and, naked as at their birth, prepared themselves for the final plunge at Te Rēinga. They faced a fence that provided an obstacle to be mounted. If they climbed over it they were able to return, but if they went under the fence they had no option but to continue their journey. The land was lost to sight as the wairua descended the far side of the hill.

Some distance south of Te Rēinga the spirits reached the famous stream Te Waiora-a-Tāne, or Te Waiorahopo. Drinking the waters of this stream destroyed all hopes of return. The spirits who did not cross the stream or drink its waters might still rejoin their bodies. Men and women who recovered from a severe illness were said to have returned from Te Waiora-a-Tāne. There may have been an ancient wairua there who assisted the spirits to cross by providing a stick or plank, or who sometimes drove them away, telling a warrior to go back to care for his family.

Spirits that came from the East Coast and passed along Takapaukura (Tom Bowling Bay) on the northern shore had to face the perils of the Kapowairua Stream, where demons snatched at them as they reached the bank.

Having passed the rivers of no return on their northern journey, the wairua reached a short beach named Te Oneirehia, ascended a slope and crossed the stream Te Waingunguru (The water of lamentation), which received its name from the sound it made as it swirled around the rocks in its steep descent. At length the highest point was reached and the spirit came to the end of the promontory and the pōhutukawa that overhung the entrance to Te Rēinga. This legendary tree has long since disappeared, though another grows in its place or a little higher on the headland. The original tree was named Aka-ki-te-rēinga (Root to the Underworld) and the red blossom Te Pua-o-te-rēinga (Flower of the spirit's flight). It was said that after Hongi's terrible raids in the 1820s, when his musket-bearing warriors spread terror throughout the northern part of Aotearoa, the branch was broken by the weight of so many passing spirits.

The wairua waited until the swirling water displaced the Rimuimōtau (Seaweed at Mōtau) and revealed the entrance, then it dropped into the clear water and reached the Underworld.

At this point there are two divergent beliefs. While it was usually said that Te Rēinga lay directly beneath the opening in the kelp, Māori also shared the common Polynesian teaching that the way of the soul led towards the setting sun. At first the wairua lingered with the body for the space of time that a baby takes to be freed from the umbilical cord. It dived under the water when it reached Te Rēinga and came to the surface again at Ōhau, one of the Three Kings Islands that may be seen from the crest of the hill at Cape Rēinga. There was a final hill to climb on the island, where the wairua chanted its mournful farewell:

Ōhau i waho rā e	Ōhau in the distance
E puke whakamutunga!	Last hill of farewell!

From there the way stretched on to the sinking sun, Te Ara-whānui-a-Tāne (The broad path laid down by Tāne), which leads to far Hawaiki, to Irihia the homeland. In that land there is a famous mountain with three different names: Maungaharo, Te Tihi-o-manono and Irirangi. This was the home of the children of Rangi and Papa and the place where sacred rites were performed to Io. At Te Honoiwairua was the renowned temple of Hawaikinui.

The spirits had to cross the river Karokaro-pounamu, assisted by the ferrywoman Rohe. When the wairua vanished beneath the water, the mihi tangata, the wailing of the innumerable dead, was heard. Doubtless they were greeting the new arrival. The wairua was invited to eat and, having done so, there could be no return.

The legends that follow tell how adventurous mortals visited the underworlds and returned to tell the tale.

Hutu and Pare

Hutu was a good-looking young man and skilful at dart-throwing. He visited a neighbouring village to take part in the games that were played during the season of amusement and of all the participants he demonstrated the most prowess.

As he took part in these sports he was unaware that he was being closely observed by Pare, a puhi (virgin) of such high rank that she was virtually kept a prisoner in her own house, surrounded by palisades and waited on by carefully selected attendants who watched over her ceaselessly.

Pare lost her heart completely to the accomplished stranger and, when near the end of the sports Hutu's dart came close to her whare, she ran swiftly from her home, picked up the small spear and carried it inside. Hutu followed her to the door and asked for his dart, but she would not give it to him unless he came inside.

This was a plain declaration of her love for him, in accordance with the custom of such aristocratic young women. However, Hutu refused, making the excuse that he feared the anger of the people if he violated her tapu. The young woman tossed her head haughtily and replied that her people would do as she told them. Hutu then confessed that he could not respond to her love, as he had a wife and two children. Overcome with shame and sorrow, Pare gave him his dart in silence, shut the door and, as soon as she was alone, killed herself.

The house remained silent for so long that at last Pare's attendants entered and found their mistress dead. Hutu had been seen talking to her. He was seized by the angry people and quickly condemned to death. He pleaded that he had not interfered with her and in fact had rejected her advances, but in vain. Seeing that there was no escape, Hutu asked if he might have three days before he was put to death. After some discussion the elders agreed to his request. He was led to a small whare and kept in solitary confinement.

Hutu, himself a rangatira, remembered the karakia that were chanted by the tohunga of his tribe at the deathbeds of ariki. He repeated them, concentrating on the most powerful spells. Soon his wairua left his body lifeless on the floor and began the journey to Te Rēinga. He passed the guardians and at length reached the spirit world, where the souls of the dead went about their daily work. He sought for the puhi and was told that she had gone into a house made ready for her, but that she refused to speak or to see any other wairua.

Remembering his prowess in the earth-life, Hutu devised a plan that would not only attract Pare's attention but also provide them both with a means of escape. Enlisting the aid of some of the young men, he lopped the branches from a tall tree until the trunk was bare. Strong plaited ropes were tied to the top and Hutu told the people to pull on them until the tree was bent in the form of a bow. Hutu and a volunteer climbed to the end of the bowed trunk and hung on firmly. At a shout the people released the ropes, the tree sprang upright, and the two men flew through the air and dropped lightly to the ground.

Everyone was excited and wanted to take part in this novel sport. The laughter and shouting brought Pare out of her whare to see what was happening. For a little while she stood watching. Then her eyes met Hutu's. She smiled and came up to him and said, 'Let me also swing on the tree; but please let me sit beside you so that I can hold close to you.'

They climbed the tree together and Pare held firmly to her loved one. 'Pull! Pull!' Hutu shouted to the people. 'Further! Let the top of the tree touch the ground!' They pulled at the ropes and the tree creaked with the strain, but eventually the top touched the ground.

'Now!' shouted Hutu. The ropes were released, the tree sprang upwards and Pare and Hutu were hurled far up towards the upper regions of Te Rēinga. Up and up they went, closer and closer to the ceiling of the Underworld, up to the roots of grass and weeds and of great trees that had grown down through the soil. Hutu caught a tree root in his hands while Pare hung round his neck. Their flight was arrested and they were able to pull themselves through cracks in the soil upwards to the world of sunlight.

Hand in hand they went through the forest until they reached Pare's village. There the two souls entered their bodies and they showed themselves, alive and well, to the people. There was great rejoicing. Hutu was pardoned and allowed to return to his own tribe.

What happened then we do not know, but the perils they had survived together evidently drew the two young people together for eventually Hutu returned and married Pare; they lived together and had many children. It is likely that Hutu retained both wives, but the new one became part of him, for he was known thereafter not as Hutu, but as Parehutu.

Putawai

Wetenga and his three closest friends went into the forest on a hunting expedition. During the afternoon he became separated from his companions. For a while they kept in touch with each other by shouting, but after some time the voices of Wetenga's friends died away in the distance.

The young man had been so engrossed looking for birds that he had paid little attention to his surroundings. He realised that he was lost. It was therefore with some relief that he heard the sound of shouting once more. He hurried towards the sound and suddenly found himself face to face with a man of unusual size, whom he had never seen before.

'Who are you?' the stranger asked.

'I am Wetenga.'

'What are you doing in this part of the forest?'

'I have lost my friends. I am looking for them now.'

'Follow me,' the stranger said. 'I will take you back to them.'

The stranger threaded his way quickly through the trees with Wetenga hard at his heels. Before long the hunter grew puzzled, for he was being led in a roundabout fashion that left him bewildered and dizzy. He caught his foot on a projecting root, stumbled and fell against the trunk of a tree. In a flash his guide whirled round, tore out a vine from the ground and bound Wetenga to the tree. He taunted the young man.

'You do not know who I am or you would not have entrusted yourself to my care. I am called Hiritoto. I am a wairua and I have need of young women for food.'

'What has that got to do with me?' Wetenga asked as he struggled against his bonds.

'You are to be the decoy, my young friend. You are a handsome man. Some girl in the pā will be sorrowful when you do not return; I fancy she will come looking for you before long.'

Wetenga shivered. He knew that what Hiritoto had said was true. He and Putawai were deeply in love with each other. When he did not return with his friends she would be sure to come in search of him.

It was a long wait. When the other hunters returned home they reassured Putawai, saying, 'No, he is not with us. We were separated, but Wetenga is a skilled hunter. Don't worry, he may have gone further than he thought. He will come back soon.'

But Wetenga did not return that night, or the next. On the third day a search party set out accompanied by Putawai. She also became separated from the others. She walked for a long way and grew tired and thirsty. She stopped to drink from a rivulet, but straightened up as she heard someone laughing.

It was Hiritoto. Without a word he seized her in one huge hand. In spite of her struggles he threw her over his shoulder and rose into the air. Flying above the treetops he came to a valley and dropped to the ground. Hiritoto, still carrying his burden, entered a deep, mysterious hole in the ground. As daylight faded Putawai lost consciousness.

She knew no more until she opened her eyes in the unusual light of Rarohenga and found that she was surrounded by wairua who had the pale skins and red hair of patupaiarehe. Hiritoto laughed again.

'What do you think of my plump little pigeon?' he asked his friends. 'Guard her well while I see to the preparation of the ovens.'

As he disappeared, an even larger and rather benevolent wairua bent over her. There was an expression of compassion in his eyes. He straightened and turned to the others.

'What are you waiting for? Hiritoto needs your help to gather firewood.'

They hurried away. He smiled encouragingly at the girl, bent over her again and untied the cords with which Hiritoto had bound her when he first brought her to the Underworld.

'My name is Manoa,' he said. 'I have no liking for the meals that Hiritoto and his friends enjoy so much. I am lonely and I would be happy to have you as my wife. Will you come with me?'

Putawai realised that Manoa was her only hope of escape and that it would be better to be the wife of a wairua than flesh cooking in an umu. She put her arms around his neck and once again she was borne through the air. They alighted at the terrible underworld home of the ngerengere (lepers). In spite of their repulsive appearance, Manoa and Putawai sheltered among them. Soon Hiritoto and his friends, angry at the loss of their prey, came flying through the air and tried to reach the fugitives. The ngerengere did their best to hinder them but they were feeble and could do little to stop them.

Manoa gathered Putawai up in his arms again and flew on until they came to the region where blind wairua were gathered. Hiritoto caught up with them and once again Manoa and Putawai had to make their escape.

They next arrived at Manoa's own pā. His people rallied to his aid and they successfully repelled Hiritoto and his followers. After Hiritoto was driven off, Manoa took Putawai to wife and she endured the strange world and the company of spirits as well as she could.

Meanwhile, when Wetenga was eventually found by his friends, he was at the door of death. Bound upright to the tree trunk, without food and water and the vines biting cruelly into his skin, he was a pitiable sight. He was released and carried back to the pā. Many weeks went by before he recovered. He was haunted by the nightmare of his loved one's capture, for he had been a witness to her abduction.

When he recovered he knew that nothing could be done to help her. She had been taken to the Underworld where no mortal could follow. When he was fully restored to strength, he joined in the work and recreation of the village and in time the memory of his sorrow grew faint. One day, however, he saw a strange woman. 'Tēnā koe,' he said. 'What is your name?'

'Putawai.'

'You cannot be Putawai. She was my lover, but she was eaten by a wairua.'

The woman came closer. 'Look at me, Wetenga. Am I not still your loved one?'

Wetenga retreated quickly. 'No, no. You are a wairua. You have come to deceive me.'

Putawai followed him and put her hand on his arm. 'Put your arms around me, Wetenga. Feel me. I am no wairua. I am still your Putawai. I have come back to you from the world of spirits.'

It was a wonderfully happy reunion when Wetenga realised that his lover had returned to him. They were joined together in marriage without delay. In the darkness of the whare she told her husband all that had happened to her in Rarohenga — all except the fact that for some months she had been the wife of the wairua Manoa.

One night Wetenga was wakened by the sound of crying. It was the wail of a newborn baby. The sound ceased abruptly. Wetenga groped in the darkness. He felt his wife's body and then the form of a baby, whose cries had been stilled when Putawai put it to her breast.

'This is my baby,' she said proudly.

'Your baby?' Wetenga asked incredulously.

'Yes. It is the baby I bore to Manoa in the Underworld. I did not tell you because I feared you would be jealous, but it can be hidden no longer.'

'Why have I not known of it? What happens to it in the daytime?'

'Have no fear, husband. Before it is light Manoa comes and takes it away. It is a wairua and has no place in the world of light.'

Wetenga was not satisfied. No man of self-respect could tolerate the constant visits of a wairua and this was what he suspected. He grasped his taiaha and sat up waiting for Manoa's arrival. However, towards morning he became drowsy and fell asleep. The same thing happened every night. Wetenga realised that it was the wairua's spells that lulled him to sleep.

When he questioned Putawai during the day, she laughed at him and told him that he had been dreaming. Indeed, the whole subject seemed too ridiculous to be true in the cold morning light. But at night-time the baby was there in the whare and Wetenga was ready to fight the wairua — until sleep came with the dawn.

This pattern continued until the baby was weaned and it could return with its father to dwell permanently in the spirit world. After this happened Wetenga's suspicions were like an evil dream that he quickly forgot and from then on he lived happily with his wife.

Tamanui-a-rangi and Rukutia

This story comes from the far south of the South Island. Tamanui-a-rangi was a man who was plain, even to the point of ugliness. He had several children, all of whom were young. It is said that he had the wanderlust and that he was addicted to searching for female slaves and stealing.

One day he was visited by a chief named Tūtekoropanga and his followers. After food had been given to the visitors the usual haka were performed. Unfortunately Tama and his people made a sorry contrast with Tūtekoropanga and his people, for the maro (kilt-like garments) of the former were made of dogs' tails while the visitors were resplendent in maro made with bright red feathers.

Tama was so ashamed that he retired to his whare and would see no one. His wife Rukutia remained on the marae, fascinated by the good looks and fine apparel of the newcomers, especially those of their leader. Tūtekoropanga noticed her and quickly made advances, which she reciprocated. 'You live with a man who has a cold and wrinkled skin,' Tūtekoropanga said. 'Come with me and I will care for you.'

While Tama remained brooding in his whare, Tū called Tama's children to him and told them that he was leaving at once with their mother. They were not to call their father but were to wait until he came outside. Then they could tell their father that his wife had left him for a more handsome husband and that he was not to attempt to follow because many obstacles would be placed in his path. By land there would be thorns and nettles, impenetrable bush and steep ravines, while in the ocean there would be monsters and whirlpools, all of which were to be created by the magic arts of Tūtekoropanga.

When Tamanui-a-rangi heard that his wife had left with Tūtekoropanga, he thought deeply. There was no doubt that his wife had been seduced by the superior charm and attractiveness of the visiting chief. He was determined to win her back, but fighting against unearthly objects would do no good, nor would it help him even if he overcame them, as he was so unattractive in appearance. As he brooded he realised that there might be a way he could make himself more attractive. Perhaps the wairua of his dead relatives in Rarohenga might help him to change his appearance.

Leaving his children behind, he set out. Presently he met a kōtuku (white heron) and changed himself into the form of this graceful bird. With slow strokes of his wings he flew down the path to Rarohenga and alighted on the lake, which is surrounded by hills.

His ancestors, Tūwhenua and Tūmaunga, and their daughter, Te Kohiwai, happened to be close by. They watched the bird. 'It is new to the lake,' Tūwhenua said. 'Look, it has eight bends in its neck. I wonder who it is.'

Tūmaunga turned to Te Kohiwai. 'Make the tamatāne charm that tells who people are,' he said. She did so and threw it at the kōtuku. The charm wound itself around the bird's neck. The young woman went up to it and brought it to her parents. The bird changed into the shape of a man and Tamanui-a-rangi stood before his relatives, who recognised him at once.

Tama could not keep his eyes off them, for they were tattooed in the manner of people of the Underworld. He realised at once that this was what he needed to restore himself to favour with his wife, and asked them if they would help him. They agreed and drew graceful whorls and spirals on his face. He looked at his reflection in the water and was delighted with his appearance, but when he bathed in the lake the marks disappeared. The moko was drawn again, but once more it washed off when Tama swam in the lake. He was annoyed.

'Why is your moko permanent, while mine is so easily destroyed?' he demanded.

'We cannot make a lasting moko here,' they explained. 'For that you would have to go to your other ancestors, Toka and Hā, who live at Tuapiko and Tūwhaitiri. They are trained in the art and have all the instruments and pigments that are needed for the permanent moko.'

Tama went on until he found these relations and made his request. They tried to dissuade him and warned him that the operation was so severe that it might result in his death. Tama pointed out that they were properly tattooed and alive. They could not deny this, but said that the pain of the operation was as bad as death. Tama was determined to secure the permanent adornment and so the experts began their work. Tama often lapsed into unconsciousness due to the pain. Once, in a lucid moment, he groaned, 'Toka! Hā! I am very bad,' but they said, 'It is not we who are hurting you. It is the chisel.'

When the work was finished he was carried into a whare and put by the fire, where he lay for some days until he had fully recovered. The plain, unattractive Tama was now a handsome warrior, and any woman would have been proud to have him for a husband.

He bathed once more in the lake to make sure that the pattern of the moko was indelible and then hurried back to his children. They were so impressed by his appearance that they gave him gifts of rotu and pūairuru (fragrant scents), and a pōkeka kiekie (a kiekie cape).

After staying with his children for a while Tama went in search of his wife. Before leaving he smeared himself with dirt and ashes, so that his moko could not be seen. He took with him his māipi (a sharp flint), and various scents, including the rotu and pūairuru, and began to tackle the obstacles that Tūtekoropanga had put in his way. He chanted karakia that caused mountains to be moved aside, and he used his māipi to cut a path through all the thorns and brambles in the dense forest.

He came to a place named Poutiri, where his slave Timuaki brought him food. Tama chanted an incantation that caused the slave to be turned into a mountain, which was named Timuaki after him. For a while Tama lived in a cave at Poutiri.

After this Tama went on alone. He met Pounamu (Greenstone), which was alive like a human. He killed and cooked it, but it burst into pieces that flew to different parts of the land, thus accounting for its later distribution.

Eventually Tama saw the ocean and recognised Tūtekoropanga's kāinga. The people of the village were cutting firewood at the edge of the forest. He went up to them and asked what they were doing. He looked so miserable and unkempt that they took him for a slave. They told him that they were gathering wood for the fires that night because Rukutia, the wife of Tūtekoropanga, would be dancing for them.

When they had finished gathering the wood they allowed Tama to accompany them. After the evening meal he sat in an inconspicuous corner of the whare tapere. There was a hush of expectation as Rukutia appeared. Tū presented her with a richly ornamented maro to tie round her waist. As she stepped into the open space between the fires, Tama quietly chanted a karakia that caused his wife to cry uncontrollably. She squatted down, wiped the tears away, and stood up. At once her tears began to flow again.

Time after time the same thing happened. The people muttered to each other, and Tū became angry, but there was nothing he could do. He shook Rukutia and struck her, but she kept on sobbing and sobbing until the fires died down and the people made ready to sleep. Tūtekoropanga at last realised that Rukutia was unable to dance and he allowed her to lie down.

Tama repeated another karakia to cause a deep sleep to fall on everyone. As soon as he was sure that he was the only one awake, he took one of the fragrant bundles from under his armpit and opened it up. A sweet smell filled the house. Rukutia sat up and exclaimed, 'Oh, the sweet smell of rotu!' She looked at Tama and asked, 'Have you come from my husband Tamanui-a-rangi?'

Tama put the rotu away and opened another bundle that gave out an offensive smell. Rukutia wrinkled her nose in disgust. Tama took out the first one again and for the second time Rukutia asked if he came from her true husband. Her voice woke Tūtekoropanga, who heard what she was saying and said roughly, 'What nonsense you talk! Tama can't possibly overcome the obstacles I have put in his path.'

Rukutia was annoyed. 'The eyes of that miserable slave reminded me of my husband,' she said coldly. Tū grunted and went to sleep and Rukutia lay down on her mat. Tama stole quietly outside. He walked down the beach until he was standing in the shallow water and washed the dirt off his face. He tied up his hair, put on his finest cloak and came and sat outside the whare.

Again he chanted a karakia that he knew would draw his wife out of

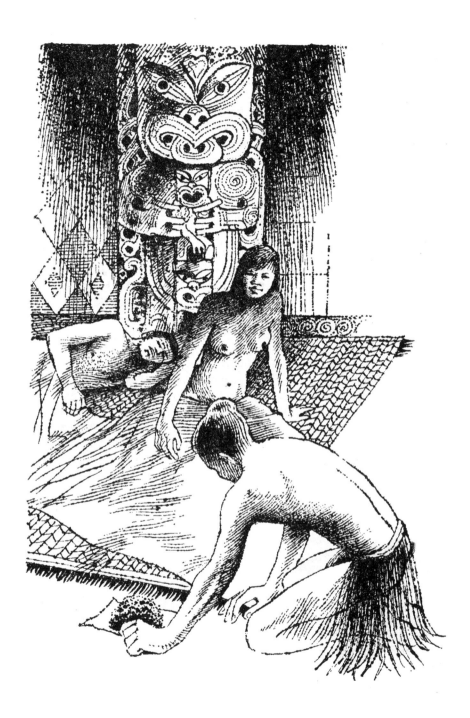

the house. Sure enough, impelled by some mysterious force, she got up, opened the door and went outside. She felt a tug at her garment and looking down she saw a handsome young man, richly tattooed and clad in a magnificent cloak, sitting with his back to the wall. She stooped and peered into his face, then drew back with a sudden cry. 'Tama — my husband!'

Tama drew her down and they talked in whispers. 'Please take me with you,' she begged. 'Tū is vindictive and rough and once he had me to himself he no longer cared for me. He ill-treats me, as you saw yourself. I know I was wrong to leave. Please take me away.'

'You preferred him to me, your husband,' Tama replied. 'It was of your own choice you left, not caring for me. You made up your own mind. Now you must stay with Tūtekoropanga.'

She bowed her head to her knees and cried silently. Tama stood up and looked down at her. 'But you must wait,' he said more gently. 'Wait patiently. One morning you will see the sail of my canoe on the water. Watch carefully every morning. When you see it, climb on the whata and call out to the people, "There is my husband Tamanui-a-rangi."'

When Rukutia looked up her husband had gone.

Tama returned to his home and prepared for the canoe voyage. He knew that Tūtekoropanga would seek the aid of taniwha and other water monsters to attack him, but the only preparation he made was to put on board a supply of ashes and some lengths of timber. His young men took their places and the canoe put out to sea.

When they reached deep water they were set upon by the taniwha. Tama scattered the ashes in the water until it became dark and the taniwha could not see. Then the timber was thrown overboard and the sail hoisted. The canoe slipped away through the waves, leaving the sea monsters to fight over the floating timber, thinking it was Tama's canoe.

They sailed on through the night and at daylight they saw land ahead. From the kāinga Rukutia saw the bright sail of the canoe and climbed on to the whata. Her cry, 'There is my husband Tamanui-a-rangi!' brought Tū's people out of their whare. They ran down to the beach as the canoe drew closer. They could see Tamanui-a-rangi standing among the paddlers. The deeply etched lines of his beautiful moko stood out clearly in the sunlight. He was clad in a cloak of bright red feathers.

'Tū!' they called. 'It is Tama!' But Tūtekoropanga did not bother to get up. He did not believe their report, for he was confident that his magic arts had closed the paths of land and sea to Tama.

Tama called to Rukutia to come to the canoe. Casting her cloak away she plunged into the water and swam towards him. He leaned over and caught her by the hair. With one swift stroke he severed her head from her body. Her body tumbled into the canoe, which turned round and sailed away.

At this time the canoe was named Whakateretere-te-ururangi (Sail towards the sunrise) because of the beauty of Tama's cloak. When the sailors reached home Tama wrapped the body of his wife in a cloak, put it in a wooden box and buried it near the wall of his house.

After this Tama was very unhappy. Day after day he sat in the house of mourning thinking of his lost wife. Winter passed and spring came. The tutu trees put out new shoots. Then one day he heard a sound of buzzing. It was a blue-bottle fly, which seemed to be singing. He listened carefully. 'U-mu, never mind my severed head, u-mu.'

Tama knew that the song had a special meaning for him. He ordered the box that held his wife's body to be raised from the ground and opened. And there was Rukutia, alive and smiling at her husband.

Hinemārama

Two orphan boys lived and grew up together. Their names were Rangirua and Kāeo and their home was a whare in a forest clearing. When they came to manhood they became conscious of their isolation and realised what a difference it would make to their lives if they had a woman to look after them.

Rangirua, the more aggressive of the two, made a journey to a nearby village and courted a young woman named Hinemārama. The girl responded quickly to his lovemaking and, with the consent of her parents, returned with him to the whare in the forest clearing. She proved to be a loving wife and looked after the brothers well.

It can be imagined what sorrow came to the young men when Hinemārama fell ill and died. The girl's relations were summoned and the tangi lasted for several days. When the brothers were alone again Rangirua gave way to his grief. His brother tried to cheer him up.

'We both miss her,' he said, 'but there are other young women who would care for us. All you have to do is to go to another kāinga and choose for yourself.'

'You will never understand,' Rangirua said. 'To you she was like a mother and a sister, but to me she was a wife. There could never be another Hinemārama.'

'If you miss her so much you should follow her to Rarohenga so that you can be with her,' Kāeo replied.

'Yes, that is what I shall do. The light is darkened in Te Ao Mārama since Hinemārama has gone.'

'If you go I shall go too,' Kāeo said.

They took three baskets of food with them for the journey into the unknown. By the time they reached Te Rēinga only one basket was left. They descended the steep hillside, hung on the branch of the ancient pōhutukawa and dropped through the writhing kelp.

There was a moment's thunder and a roaring of water in their ears before they fell unconscious. When they woke they found themselves in a strange land. There were trees, grasses and ferns, and a deep, swiftly flowing river in front of them. They walked along the riverbank and presently met an old woman.

'Haere mai! Haere mai e ngā manuhiri!' she said, believing them to be spirits who had come to begin their long sojourn in Rarohenga. 'What is your tribe?'

'Ngāpuhi.'

'Then you are welcome. But a few days ago I took a young woman of Ngāpuhi to her home here.'

'What was her name?' Rangirua asked eagerly.

'It was Hinemārama.'

'She is my wife. Where is she?'

'She has crossed the river. You will find her in the kāinga over there among the trees.'

'How can we cross the river?'

'If you go further along the bank and call, the ferryman will come to you.'

The brothers thanked her and went some distance downstream until they could see the whare of the kāinga behind the trees. They called until they saw a canoe leave the opposite bank and come towards them. It was small and was paddled by a spirit of unprepossessing appearance.

'Hasten!' he said abruptly. 'There is much work for me to do. I have no time to wait.'

'Your canoe is too small to hold us both,' Rangirua said. 'You will have to take one of us and come back for the other.'

The ferryman showed his annoyance. 'Do you think you can tell me what to do?' he asked angrily. 'Spirits weigh lightly. This canoe has carried many men and women in one load. When a battle has been fought they crowd here in their thousands.'

Rangi and Kāeo looked at one another out of the corner of their eyes. They were in danger of being detected as mortals by the ferryman.

'I would rather cross by myself,' Rangirua said quickly. 'Take my brother with you and I will swim across.'

Before the ferryman had time to object, Kāeo stepped into the canoe and Rangirua pushed it away from the bank. Still grumbling, the ferryman took up his paddle as Rangi slipped into the water and began to swim across the river. He reached the far side nearly as quickly as the canoe. The brothers walked up to the kāinga together.

The people of the kāinga crowded around them. Among them they recognised their father, Pākira, and their mother, Toretū. Standing behind them was Hinemārama. They wept over one another and mingled their tears. As soon as he could Rangirua took Hinemārama to one side. Her eyes were shining.

'How is it that you have come to me so quickly?' she asked.

'I have come to take you away, back to your home.'

Her face fell. 'Husband, we are spirits. We can never return to Te Ao Mārama.'

'Wife, you are wrong! Kāeo and I are not spirits. We have eluded the guardians and have come to you as men. Take us into your whare. We must not attract attention.'

When they had gone inside they revealed their secret to their mother and father. Toretū said, 'Are you hungry after your long journey? Sit down and partake of your first meal in Rarohenga.'

She put food in front of them, but her sons drew back in disgust. The food was nauseating and had an evil smell.

'Do not eat it,' Pākira said in alarm. 'If you taste it you will never return to the world of light.'

'Have no fear,' Rangi said. 'We have brought food with us from the cultivations of men.'

He opened the basket of kūmara. Toretū's eyes filled with tears.

'They remind me of our happy days when we lived with our relatives and our sons were little children. After eating the food of the wairua we can no longer eat the food of humans. Eat, my sons, and give some to Hinemārama. She has been with us for such a short time that she has not yet eaten with us.'

After the meal they went outside and farewelled their parents and the other relatives who had gathered to greet them on their arrival. Then Rangirua and Hinemārama went to the riverbank and sat down in the canoe.

'What are you doing?' the ferryman asked in surprise.

'We want you to take us back to the other side of the river.'

'No one goes there. My task is to bring spirits across to this side. The wairua who come to Rarohenga never return.'

'But I am not a spirit. I am a man.'

The ferryman caught his shoulder and ran his hands down his arms and legs and patted his stomach.

'Yes, you are a man!' he said. 'You have no right to be in this place. I will take you across. You must hurry away and never return.'

When they reached the far bank, Rangirua stepped ashore and held out his hand to help Hinemārama.

'The woman stays with me. She is a wairua,' the ferryman said.

'She has not eaten the food of the Underworld,' Rangirua protested. 'She is my wife. She comes with me.'

Hine caught her husband's hand and began to scramble out of the canoe, but the ferryman caught her by the ankle. There was a tug of war between them. Rangi was joined by Kāeo, who had swum the river, and together they pulled while Rangi raised his foot and pushed the prow of the canoe. In danger of losing his balance, the ferryman released his hold and Hine was pulled safely to shore.

The three fugitives ran up the bank of the river. They met the old woman who peered at them with rheumy eyes and croaked, 'You are going back for more? Good. I will show you the way.'

They hurried past her, and climbed up to the surging waters and the endlessly moving kelp. Through it they could see the glorious sunshine. There was another moment of cold and confusion. The brothers kept a firm hold on Hinemārama and then they heard the splashing of waves and felt the warm kiss of the sun and the wind.

Back at their whare one thing remained to be done. Hinemārama was neither wairua nor woman. 'You must dig up my body,' she told her husband. 'It must be washed and then my spirit will enter the dead flesh and I shall be alive once more and your wife forever.'

And it was so.

PATUPAIAREHE

In traditional times there was a widespread belief in the existence of the patupaiarehe, a supernatural people who lived in dense forests and on the cloud-wreathed summits of mountains. They were supposed to inhabit fortified villages made of the vines of the kareao (supplejack). When they ventured out of their pā, they chose wet or misty days so as not to be seen. They were feared and were considered dangerous.

Although descriptions varied, patupaiarehe were often described as having fair skin and long red hair. They were not tattooed and wore white garments. Patupaiarehe mothers carried their babies in their arms instead of holding them on their hips.

They ate raw forest foods and raw fish. People would leave offerings of fish for the patupaiarehe as a precautionary measure, to prevent them from driving away the local fish.

Patupaiarehe were known by a number of different names including tūrehu, heketoro, kōrakorako, nanakia, tahurangi, pākehakeha and tutumaio. Ponaturi (sea fairies), porotai (stone people) and maero (ferocious forest creatures) also had many things in common with patupaiarehe.

There is a story of their arrival on the Tainui canoe; another story says that they were placed in their mountain retreats by Ngātoroirangi of Te Arawa canoe; yet another story says that some are descended from Tama-o-hoi, the atua of Tarawera, who divided that mountain from Ruawāhia.

Some have proposed that stories of patupaiarehe are based on memories of fair-skinned people encountered long ago by the ancestors in distant lands. Others say that they were the remnant of the earliest inhabitants of Aotearoa, who were displaced from their lands and took refuge in the remote parts of the forest.

The ghostly piping of their kōauau and pūtōrino (types of flute) and the sound of fairy songs could often be heard in the misty forest heights. The songs were sometimes collected line by line, for people could not remember more than a single line at a time. One such waiata from Banks Peninsula was recorded by James Cowan in *Maori Folk Tales of the Port Hills*:

Tītī whakatai aro rua
E hoki rā koe
Ki Ōtepātātū
Ki te pā whakatangi
Ki te kōauau
Ki tauwene ai
I raro i au e!

O tītī, bird of the sea
Bird of the hilltop cave
Come back to Ōtepātātū
To the lofty dwelling
Where the sweet sounds are heard
The sound of the fairy flute
The music of the mountains
That thrilled me through and through!

The plaintive notes of their kōauau and pūtōrino sometimes exercised a fatal attraction to young women who, in spite of many warnings, were lured to the homes of the patupaiarehe. Light-haired people, called urukehu, were supposed to be the descendants of such unions.

The fairies of Te Urewera were supposed to be gentle, retiring folk, but elsewhere they used their magic powers to terrify mortals, the patupaiarehe men carrying women off to their homes and the fairy women luring men to their destruction. Those who were abducted seldom returned, but lived in a dazed condition among their supernatural captors.

The patupaiarehe of the Whanganui River were said to gather in large numbers among the kūmara cultivations and hold their kōrero (discussions) there. They never damaged the crops. At other times they became invisible and it was only the matakite (seers) who could see them. They entered the wharepuni (sleeping houses) and afflicted the occupants, sending them into a coma. The unconscious sufferers were taken outside and drenched with water in order to revive them.

Fortunately there were two defences against patupaiarehe. These were cooked food and kōkōwai, the red ochre that was a sacred colour to Māori. Their eschewing of cooked food points to their being wairua or spirits of the dead. Examples of the use of these unconventional weapons appear in many stories.

Patupaiarehe generally shunned sunlight and came out only when the mist lay heavy on the hills. According to Ngāti Whātua the long lava flow called Meola Reef, which extends for some distance across the upper Waitematā Harbour near Point Chevalier, was the work of a travelling party of patupaiarehe. Their progress north was blocked by the upper reaches of the Waitematā. During the hours of darkness they worked furiously to build a causeway across the water. However, day dawned before they had completed their task and they had to leave the causeway unfinished.

Īhenga and the Patupaiarehe

Īhenga, the great Te Arawa ancestor, explorer and name-giver of the thermal region, came first to Rotoiti (The small lake) and then to Rotorua or, to give it its full name, Roto-rua-a-Īhenga (The second lake of Īhenga). Travelling around its shores, Īhenga reached the stream and the mountain that later became known as Ngongotahā.

Īhenga was curious to know whether the plume that drifted so lazily from the hilltop was smoke or mist. Leaving his wife in the canoe he landed and began to struggle up the slopes of the mountain. He was not daunted by the plaintive songs that rose and fell in the dripping forest, but from the corner of his eye he saw strange forms and movements that showed that he was being followed.

A breath of wind tore the mist away from the mountain peak, exposing the palisades of a pā and, closer at hand, a tree that was blazing like a torch. Īhenga broke off a branch that was alive with flame. There was a shout and pale forms rushed towards him. Īhenga swung the crackling branch around in a fiery yellow circle, which caused the patupaiarehe to retreat. He plunged it into the bracken, filling the air with choking smoke and stinging sparks. The patupaiarehe were driven back and Īhenga fled down the hillside to rejoin his wife.

Later he settled by the Waiteti Stream on the lower slopes of the mountain. He decided to try to establish friendly relations with the elusive, white-skinned people whose fairy music echoed so hauntingly through

the forest when rain and mist enveloped the mountain. He chose a day when there were no clouds. He left his pā and climbed upwards, but the undergrowth and fern impeded his progress. He grew tired and thirsty. He looked for water but there were no streams on the hill.

He was nearing the summit when, on parting the branches of the trees, he found himself in a clearing. Through the leaves he saw the palisades of the pā again, with whare and whata behind them and, moving among them, many people who were unnaturally fair of skin and whose hair was red. He called to them and they came running towards him, speaking in a language that was not his but strangely like it, so he was able to understand what they were saying.

He asked for water and a beautiful young woman offered him a drink from a calabash with a wooden mouthpiece. It was a gracious act, for water was scarce in the pā. The nearest spring was at some distance, near the Kauae spur, and water had to be brought up to the pā. Īhenga drank deeply from the calabash while the patupaiarehe crowded around him and commented on his appearance. The mountain was later named after this incident. 'Ngongo' means 'to drink', and 'tahā' is a calabash or gourd.

The strange inhabitants of Te Tūāhu-a-te-atua (The sacred place of the god) on the summit of Ngongotahā detained Īhenga. They plied him with questions and touched his body. At first Īhenga had been too overcome with amazement to take any action, but as he noticed their peculiar appearance and felt the unearthly atmosphere of the pā, he grew afraid.

He broke away from them, slipped through the palisades and hurtled down the hillside. In a moment the patupaiarehe were streaming after him. His terror gave wings to his feet. Gradually he drew away from the shouting throng. But one of them kept almost at his heels. It was the young woman who had offered him her calabash. She threw her garments away to leave her limbs unhampered and raced after him. In spite of her beauty, he knew that if she captured him she would rob him of his memory and he would never see his wife again.

In his desperation Īhenga remembered that the patupaiarehe were repelled by kōkōwai and that the smell of oil and cooked food was repugnant to them. In a pocket in his belt he kept a small piece of kōkōwai mixed with shark oil. Without faltering in his headlong pace he drew it out and smeared it over his body.

With a cry that had in it sadness and longing as well as frustration, the comely girl from the fairy pā gave up her pursuit. When Īhenga looked back he saw her standing motionless among the trees. It was a fortunate escape for the explorer, who afterwards treated the ghostly inhabitants of the forest with respect. In the years that followed there was an uneasy truce between them.

Through the generations the people who lived in the Whakaeke-tahuna pā that their ancestor Īhenga built by the Waiteti Stream often heard the piping voices of the fairies and learned their songs. The human population grew, their canoes plied the lake, and smoke and steam from umu (ovens) rose from many kāinga. War parties made trails, bird hunters penetrated far into the forest and even the tamariki (children) sometimes ventured up the slopes of Ngongotahā. Fire destroyed the dense bush and gradually the patupaiarehe were forced from their mountain home.

A final migration of the ghostly inhabitants of Ngongotahā was led by their chief Tongakohu, some going to Moehau (Cape Colville) and others to Pirongia. The lament of Tongakohu has been preserved by Te Arawa (translated here by James Cowan):

> E muri ahiahi
> Ka hara mai te aroha
> Ka ngau i ahau
> Ki taku urunga tapu
> Ka mahue i ahau
> I Ngongo' maunga
> Ka tū kau noa rā
> Te Ahi-a-Mahuika
> Nāna i tahu mai, i
> Ka haere ai au ki Moehau
> Ki Pirongia rā e
> I te urunga tapu e
> E te Rotokohu e!
> Kia āta akiaki kia mihi ake au

Ki taku tūāhu ka mahue iho nei
He rā kotahi hoki e
E noho i au
Ka haere atu ai e
Kāore e hoki mai, na-a-i.

Night's shadows fall
Keen sorrow eats my heart
Grief for the land I'm leaving
For my sacred sleeping-place
The home pillow I'm leaving
On Ngongo's lofty peak
So lone my mountain stands
Swept by the flames of Mahuika
I'm going far away
To the heights of Moehau, to Pirongia
To seek another home
O Rotokohu, leave me yet awhile
Let me farewell my forest shrine
The tūāhu I'm leaving
Give me but one more day
Just one more day and then I'll go
And I'll return no more.

Ruru

Ruru and his friend Kareawa went to a stream to catch eels. They were equipped with strips of akeake, a hardwood, with which to stun the tuna. They waded down the bed of the stream until they came to a deep hole where they could see several eels swimming lazily under the bank. Ruru drove them towards his companion, who killed them and threw them on the bank. There were only four eels in the pool and they accounted for them all.

When they came to the next pool they were somewhat surprised to find that it was inhabited by the same number of eels, which they dispatched quickly. Kareawa was disturbed by the coincidence and confessed to Ruru that he thought they must have come across a storehouse of the patupaiarehe, who were keeping the same number of eels in each pool. Ruru laughed at his fears, but Kareawa was filled with a sense of foreboding. After some argument the two men parted company, Kareawa returning to the place where they had left their clothes and Ruru continuing the hunt.

At the next pool Ruru felt a tingle of apprehension when he looked down through the clear water and saw four white tuna lying against the bank. His fear was only momentary. He caught one and hastened back to Kareawa, shouting eagerly, 'See what I have caught!'

Kareawa exclaimed with surprise when he saw the white eel, but when he heard that there were four of them, it was too much for him.

'You must put it back in the water,' he said earnestly. 'A white eel must surely be the property of the patupaiarehe and the fact that you have found four tuna for the third time proves it. If you anger the fairy people we will be in great trouble, Ruru.'

Ruru laughed. 'I am going to eat it now,' he said. In spite of his friend's protests he kindled a fire, roasted the eel and ate it. Kareawa sat at a little distance from him and, much as he loved the rich flesh of the tuna, he would take none of the tidbits that Ruru offered him.

Leaving Kareawa at their camp, Ruru continued the hunt. At the next pool there were no eels, nor at the next. In fact every pool was empty and Ruru laughed to himself at the thought of Kareawa's face.

After a while he came to a tributary, which he followed to its source, but no tuna were to be found in the stream. The evening was closing in and already it was dusk under the overhanging trees. Ruru realised that his search had taken him further away from the encampment than he had intended. It occurred to him that he could save time by going through the forest in a direct line towards the campsite.

After he had been travelling for some time the ground became rough and his path was impeded by tātarāmoa (bush lawyer) and clinging vines. He could not hear the murmur of the stream and, although he strained his eyes, there was no sign of Kareawa's campfire. He shouted, hoping to attract his friend's attention. From far away there was an answering shout, but to his surprise it came from behind. Ruru could hardly believe that he had lost all sense of direction. He shouted several times, but the answer always came from behind him. He turned round and retraced his steps, but by this time he was weary. He bumped into trees and jagged stumps and his skin was torn by the brambles.

He stumbled into a clearing and was immediately surrounded by white forms, which laid taloned fingers on him and carried him swiftly away to their hilltop pā. There they induced him to fall into a comatose state and subjected him to many indignities. They rubbed him with the palms of their hands and the soles of their feet, and made moss or lichen grow from his skin and cover his body, except for his head. His hair fell out and he became completely bald. He could not eat the raw flesh of eels and birds the patupaiarehe provided for him. After he had been held captive for a while they let him roam through the forest in search of berries.

Meanwhile, back at their village Kareawa had waited in vain for his friend to return on the night of the eeling expedition. In the morning he went along the banks of the stream calling to him. He found the three white tuna that Ruru had left, but there was no sign of his friend. Regretfully he returned to the kāinga and told everyone what had happened, giving it as his opinion that Ruru had offended the patupaiarehe and that he must have been captured by them and killed.

The beautiful Tangiroa, Ruru's wife, was inconsolable. She lacerated her breasts with sharp shells and the tears that ran down her face mingled with the blood on her body. She remained faithful to Ruru's memory for many months, but as the seasons went by he was forgotten by his people and Tangiroa's grief abated. Kareawa waited patiently. When he saw that Tangiroa was no longer mourning for her husband he declared his love for her and asked her to marry him.

Although Kareawa was a tūtūā, a person of low birth, he was young and handsome and Tangiroa would no doubt have accepted his proposal if it had not been that Maringirangi, a chief and tohunga, was also courting her. Maringirangi was old and wrinkled and his fighting days were over, but he was of aristocratic lineage, was wise and powerful, and knew how to flatter a young woman. Tangiroa hesitated in her choice. She would have turned to the older and more experienced man if another woman had not complicated matters.

Urunga was also beautiful and she was younger than Tangiroa. She had fallen in love with Kareawa and made no secret of her longing for him. Tangiroa's worst instincts were roused. At the thought that another woman had succeeded in diverting the young lover's attentions, even momentarily, her jealousy knew no bounds. She informed Kareawa at once that he possessed her heart and that she was prepared to become his wife.

Maringirangi was furious at the affront to his mana of being dismissed so summarily. He uttered a dark threat that caused much gossip and some dread in his tribe: 'There are four persons in this matter. There is the wahine, Tangiroa; there is the tūtūā, Kareawa; there is the tohunga, Maringirangi; and there is the tāne, Ruru, who was taken by the patupaiarehe. Tangiroa is nobody; Kareawa is nobody; who can tell where Ruru may be? There remains Maringirangi and the patupaiarehe, and the matter lies between them.'

It was such a sinister, bloodcurdling threat that tribal opinion turned against Tangiroa and Kareawa, and their marriage was postponed until it was seen what would happen.

A few days later Maringirangi went to the seashore and wove spells of peculiar intensity, after which he lay down to sleep. When he woke he found a stranger sitting beside him. The tohunga looked at him closely but could not recognise him. The man was naked and was covered from head to foot with a curious moss-like growth, in which the bald crown of his head lay like a polished boulder.

Maringirangi plied him with questions, seeking to know who he was and from what tribe he came, but the peculiar stranger made no reply. The tohunga thought he must be some subnormal being or madman. He peered at him more closely and saw, beneath the tufted growth, the brown skin of a Māori and the incisions of the moko.

'You are a man,' he said.

At last the stranger spoke. 'I am Ruru,' he said.

The tohunga smiled. 'Ah, Ruru, I am not surprised. Through my magic you have escaped from the patupaiarehe. Come with me.'

He led Ruru, who was still dazed and uncertain in speech and gait, along the beach and through the gates of the kāinga. A cry of horror rose from the women. 'A madman!' they cried and fled to the shelter of their whare; but Maringirangi reassured them.

'Do not be afraid,' he said. 'He is not a madman. This is our old companion Ruru. Come closer and see for yourselves. Call Tangiroa and tell her that her husband has been rescued from the clutches of the patupaiarehe and has come to claim her once again as his wife.'

Tangiroa ran towards them but recoiled when she saw the bald-pated, lichen-covered travesty of a man who stood next to the tohunga. She buried her face in her hands and wept bitterly as Maringirangi led Ruru up to her.

'Here is your reward, Tangiroa,' he said with an evil smile. 'Welcome your lover and your husband.'

But once Maringirangi had had time to reflect his heart softened towards the young woman who had once briefly claimed his affection. He reflected that he had wiped out the insult that had been offered when Tangiroa rejected him in favour of Kareawa. His better nature prevailing, he asked for warm water and, with appropriate incantations, he washed

Ruru thoroughly. The kohukohu (moss) came away freely, revealing the handsome figure of Ruru, restored to his former glory.

To his dying day Ruru carried a memento of his unhappy experiences, for his skull remained as smooth and polished as a water-worn boulder in the stream in which he had taken the tuna of the patupaiarehe.

The Patupaiarehe of the Tākitimu Mountains

Hautapu was a tohunga and bird-hunter who lived on the shores of Lake Manapōuri. He had left his home and had climbed far up the slopes of the Tākitimu mountains. There, in a sheltered valley, he had set up snares for the kōtuku (white heron) and the whio (blue duck). He was about to enter his roughly made wharau when he saw a gleam of white among the undergrowth.

He turned in a flash, leapt across the grass and, with his mere quivering in his hand, pounced on the unknown animal. As he thrust the leaves back he stopped, the mere dropping from his hand and swinging by its flax loop from his wrist. Both hands fell on to the gleaming white shoulders of a young woman, who looked up at him with frightened eyes through masses of red hair.

She had sunk to her knees. Hautapu raised her to her feet and gazed with admiration at the whiteness of her skin, her rounded limbs and well-formed body. He chuckled and drew her out into the open.

'A wife for Hautapu!' he exclaimed delighted. 'Who are you? Where are your people? Why are you white like the kōtuku?'

The girl hung her head. 'I am alone,' she said. 'I have no tribe. My home is in the mountains.'

'Sit there,' Hautapu commanded, pushing her into the wharau. He paced backwards and forwards. She must be a patupaiarehe, he decided. White body, red hair, no tribe — but why should I be frightened of a helpless woman like this? She can speak our tongue. Yet harm may come to me and my tribe if I take her now. It would be safer to let her go.

But she is more desirable than any young woman of my hapū. If I took her to wife I would tame her and she would bear me strong children. But then she does not belong to the world of men and women. She may be a wairua, a kēhua. Yet I am a tohunga. Maybe I can overcome her spirit powers. There is only one way to know. I will put it to the test now.

'What is your name?' he asked.

'Kaiheraki.'

'You will be my wife. But, before we leave this place, I must avert the evil that might come between us.'

The fairy woman said nothing. She looked at him with lingering fear still in her eyes.

Hautapu began kindling the sacred fire in preparation for the tāwhakamoe rite. He laid the kauati (lower fire-making stick) on the ground and told Kaiheraki to put her foot on it. He knelt in front of her and rubbed the kaunati (upper fire-making stick) along the groove, backwards and forwards. Smoke curled up lazily and Kaiheraki drew back with a cry, for this was an unknown thing to the patupaiarehe.

'Keep your foot there, woman,' Hautapu said angrily.

She put her foot back on the stick and held it there while the wood smoked and sparks began to glow in the groove of the kauati. One of the sparks flew out and fell on her foot. The blood flowed out where the flesh was charred and in terror the girl fled into the forest.

Hautapu raced after her, caught her and brought her back to his camp. He put damp moss on her foot and set to work once more, taking no notice of the violent tremors that shook Kaiheraki's body. He was engrossed in his task. A tiny flame appeared and he fanned it to a blaze, turning away to kindle the sacred fire.

If he had been more tender towards her she might have been delivered from her supernatural powers and have become a fitting wife for a tohunga. Who can tell? Hautapu was absorbed in his work. The tāwhakamoe rite had to be observed carefully in order to ward off the powers of witchcraft and evil.

His back was towards Kaiheraki as the fire burned up with a steady, smokeless flame. He turned back and found that the white girl of his desiring was gone.

All day he searched the valley and the slopes of the hills, calling her name. The fire burned up and died down, the embers grew dull. A gust of wind brightened them for a moment. Then rain pattered down, making black pockmarks on the glowing heap, which slowly died, turned black and glistened in the falling rain. It was nearly dark when Hautapu returned, tired, scratched and bruised. He stood for a moment looking at the sodden ashes of his fire and then threw himself down in the wharau he had built that morning.

The next day the hills were swathed in mist. Hautapu gloomily removed the birds that had been caught in the snares and took them back to his kāinga. The great prize had escaped him; he never saw Kaiheraki again. It is said that Kaiheraki haunts the Tākitimu Range and sometimes her ghost can be seen as the mists slide across the ridges and curl down into the gullies and ravines of the mountains.

Kaumariki

The famous bone fish-hook called Te Rama, after its maker, had passed from one generation to another and had become the prized possession of Kariri. It attracted fish from a distance and was never known to fail. With the passing years it had become tapu and transmitted the mana of its maker to its present owner.

One night the sacred fish-hook was stolen by three men: Kaumariki, Tāwhai and Kupe. They knew that Kariri would not rest until the thieves were discovered and the heirloom restored to him and so, while it was still dark, they launched their canoe and paddled out to sea. Long before the theft was discovered they were out of sight of land. They went on and on and after the fourth day they reached a lonely island, the waters of which teemed with fish.

'See,' said Kaumariki, as they beached the canoe, 'Te Rama is already at work. The fish are leaping to it.'

During the day he collected a large heap of firewood, but Tāwhai and Kupe had thought of a better way of keeping out the cold night air, even though it was winter. They lay down, wrapped themselves in their cloaks and heaped the dry, sun-warmed sand over their bodies.

Night was falling as Kaumariki looked at his friends. He laughed loudly. 'You are like men who have been buried,' he jeered. 'The sand will grow cold before dawn comes. A fire is the only way a man can drive away the demons of the cold.'

He dragged the brushwood and logs around to make a circle, kindled a fire and lay down in the centre. Every now and again he had to rise to put more wood on the dwindling fire. A doubt rose in his mind as to whether his companions, who were already fast asleep, might not have been more sensible. Eventually he too fell asleep.

In the middle of the night he woke with a start. The cries of terror-stricken men rang in his ears. He gazed across the dull embers of the fire and saw a sight that froze the blood in his veins. Tāwhai and Kupe, imprisoned in their sandy bed, were being attacked by ponaturi. They had the shape of men, but their skins glowed a pallid white in the dim light. Their hair was red and their fingers terminated in long, evil claws, with which they were rending the skin of Kaumariki's friends. He could do nothing to help them for he knew that the attackers were not mortal. Feverishly he piled dry wood on the fire, driving back the bolder ones who were coming towards him.

It was the longest night that Kaumariki had ever spent. As soon as the flames died down the white, loathsome creatures stretched out their arms towards him, retreating only as the frantic man fed the flames. All the time Kaumariki's gaze was fixed on his friends, whose bodies were being torn apart and eaten in front of him. Only at daybreak did the sea creatures disappear. All that was left to show where his friends had been were two shallow trenches in the sand.

Kaumariki dared not face another night on the haunted island. He ran the canoe into the water and headed homewards, dreading the anger of Kariri less than the supernatural creatures who had devoured his companions. On arriving at the pā he gave Te Rama back to its owner and addressed the tribe, admitting his offence and telling of everything that had happened to him. In view of what he had suffered his theft was pardoned.

'I am determined to avenge the death of my friends,' he declared. 'Who will come with me? I need a hundred warriors with food for all and several waka taua to convey us to the island.'

'How will you overcome the ponaturi?' he was asked. 'They are powerful and might easily defeat an ope, for there is a great horde of them.'

'I have laid my plans,' was the reply. 'If you do what I tell you, we will defeat them. The women must collect supplies of raupō leaves and mānuka stakes to provide materials for a large whare. Then I require many tree trunks to be cut and fashioned into the shape of people, and garments with which to clothe them.'

While the preparations were being made, Kaumariki went away by

himself and made four lamps from gourds, which he packed with absorbent fungus and filled with shark oil. Each gourd was provided with a cylindrical cover of bark so its light could be hidden.

Six canoes sailed across the ocean, conveying the warriors and all the material that had been assembled for their expedition. As soon as they disembarked everyone set to work to build a large wharepuni. The wooden effigies, wrapped in cloaks, were placed on the sleeping mats. Kaumariki suspended the lamps from the four corners of the house with a warrior in charge of each. When night came the subdued light from the shielded lamps illuminated the interior of the whare and it seemed as though many people were sleeping there.

The remaining warriors sheltered behind a circle of fire outside the whare. The hours passed slowly but everyone was alert. Towards midnight a whisper passed through the ranks of the warriors. A dark shadow had appeared out of the water. As it advanced up the beach, the white skin and red hair of the ponaturi reflected the leaping flames. It was joined by three more figures. The four scouts, keeping well away from the fires, approached the whare. They peered through the open doorway, saw the bodies lying motionless and said, 'Kei te moe!' (They're asleep!) Their leader came forward, looked inside and repeated, 'Āe, kei te moe.'

Then scores of ponaturi rushed up the beach, flooded through the doorway and fell on the bodies that lay so still on the mats. As soon as they were all inside Kaumariki shouted. The four men who had remained inside the whare pulled the shades from the lamps. In the sudden glare of light the ponaturi were blinded. Hiding their faces in their hands they rushed to and fro, bumping into each other and vainly seeking the doorway. In the confusion the four warriors made their escape.

As soon as they emerged Kaumariki barred the door and torches were applied to the brushwood walls. There was a bright gleam of flame and a swirling cloud of smoke. Then the whare grew bright in the blaze of light as the flames licked the walls and snatched at the thatched roof. In the fiercely blazing whare the ponaturi were burned to death as Kaumariki avenged the murder of his companions, Tāwhai and Kupe.

TANIWHA

Taniwha occupy a special place in Māori mythology. They were ferocious beasts who devoured lazy children and brave warriors alike. Many dwelt in water but some lived in caves. Some could travel underground and others could fly. It took many warriors and a lot of cunning to trap and kill a taniwha.

Some taniwha could be placated with the appropriate karakia and gifts of food. Even those taniwha who had a special relationship with a tribe and acted as guardians were known to turn bad if the supply of tribute, usually in the form of choice foodstuffs, was interrupted.

Taniwha were often called ngārara (lizards). Native lizards, all small in size, were symbols of death and evoked superstitious fear because they were omens of evil, so the idea of large, lizard-like creatures was equally as frightening to grown men as to children. There has been speculation that the legendary monsters of Aotearoa derived from stories of large lizards in tropical lands handed down over the generations.

Other taniwha were more like fish or whales. Ocean-dwelling taniwha were known to rescue those stranded on islands and to escort voyaging canoes.

According to one whakapapa, taniwha are descended from the union of Tāne and Hine-tūpari-maunga. Their daughter Pūtoto married Takaaho and they had Tuarangaranga, from whom all taniwha descend.

Sometimes taniwha are ancestors who appear in human whakapapa (genealogies). Some people, either through their own misdeeds or simply through misfortune, were turned into taniwha. Some taniwha could talk and a number had a predilection for taking human women for wives.

The stories that follow provide examples of the appearance and behaviour of these strange, supernatural creatures.

Hotupuku

A suspicion was steadily growing that some danger lurked between lakes Rotorua and Taupō. When travellers from the Taupō region did not return from a trip to Rotorua, it was thought at first that they had prolonged their stay. However, when visitors from the Rotorua region travelled south, taking an unusual route past lakes Tarawera and Rotomahana, and reached their destination, they informed their hosts that no one from the Taupō region had been seen in their district.

'Which way did you come?' they were asked.

'We came by the open plain of Kāingaroa, by the path to Tāuhunui.'

There was an animated kōrero that night. It seemed unlikely that the missing people from the Taupō region had taken the same route as their Rotorua friends. It was suspected that they had been ambushed by an unknown enemy. The hot-tempered toa were eager for revenge and the older rangatira were equally ready to take the lead. The tohunga consulted the omens and repeated that the gods favoured their enterprise. A strong taua was assembled, each village contributing its quota of warriors. Soon the expedition was on the trail. By the end of the second day they reached the northern end of Lake Taupō, crossed the Waikato River and travelled over the Kāingaroa Plains until they came to Kapenga.

Unknown to the warriors this was the home of the taniwha Hotupuku, who had waylaid and devoured their relatives. As the taua travelled across the plain, the scent of humans reached the nostrils of Hotupuku. He sprang out of his cave and bounded on them, catching them unawares. On the open plain they had taken no precautions against ambush and their weapons were not ready. It is not to be wondered at that the seasoned warriors fled in confusion, for Hotupuku had the appearance of a moving mountain. The spines and excrescences on his back had the horrid appearance of growths on a monster of the ocean.

Some of the retreating warriors were trampled to death, while others were seized in the cavernous mouth of Hotupuku and swallowed whole. However, there were so many in the war party that Hotupuku was unable to deal with them all. For several days those who had escaped the monster came stumbling into the kāinga of their friends at Rotorua, supplying further details of the catastrophe.

The Rotorua toa immediately gathered up their weapons and formed a taua 140-men strong. They journeyed to Kapenga without delay. On the way they had discussed their plan of campaign and were soon at work stripping the leaves of the tī kōuka, plaiting and twisting them into strong ropes.

The monster remained hidden in his cave while the orations that precede a battle were performed by the rangatira. It was probably still digesting the earlier meal of Taupō warriors. One of the most experienced chiefs said: 'Listen to me. Let us go gently to work. Let us not go too near to the monster, but stay at a distance from him. The wind is blowing towards him, and if we get too close he will smell us. We have been told how big he is; if he takes us unawares he will destroy us because of his size. Let us wait until the wind blows towards us from the taniwha. Then we may creep up unperceived and our preparations can be made without fear of discovery.'

His advice was taken. They waited until the wind veered in the right direction before climbing stealthily up to the cave. They could hear the monster's noisy snoring, from which it was evident he was still asleep. The rope snares were arranged at some distance from the cave, and a party of men took up positions at the sides of the entrance. They were armed with a variety of thrusting and cutting weapons. Others held the ropes, while a third party, comprised of the youngest and boldest of the warriors, stood at the mouth of the cave to lure the taniwha out into the open. They advanced cautiously towards the dark entrance. Before they had taken many steps they heard a rumbling sound, the ground shook and the huge form of Hotupuku filled the dark mouth of the cave. Not a man retreated. Some even advanced closer, enticing the taniwha to attack them.

Hotupuku roared with delight. He came forward at a run, his jaws distended, his long tongue darting from side to side in vicious strokes as he endeavoured to seize the foolhardy men. As the taniwha came out into the full light of day the men retreated, stepping carefully. The ropes lay on the ground, seemingly scattered at random, but in fact every one had been placed with care and the warriors took pains not to disturb them.

They began to run towards a small hill. Hotupuku quickened his steps as he lumbered down the slope. His fierce eyes and snapping jaws and the enormous bulk of his body were an awesome sight. But the men of Te Arawa were not afraid. They ran up the hill and remained on the top, waving their arms and taunting the taniwha. The infuriated beast climbed up after them and planted his feet firmly in the strong noose that had been prepared on the hilltop.

A sudden shout startled him. The noose sprang from the ground as a score of hands pulled the ropes. Hotupuku's front legs were caught together in a crushing grip. Like living things, other ropes circled around his legs and across his back. They wove themselves around his neck and jaws, falling lightly at first but then biting cruelly into his flesh. The excited warriors poured in on him from every side, while those who had lured him out of his cave turned back to join in the attack. Only the giant tail was free. Hotupuku lashed it from side to side, sweeping men off their feet, but it felt the bite of mere and taiaha and sharp cutting instruments.

Maddened with pain the monster reared and strained against the ropes, but he was stung and tortured still more by the weapons. The nooses were pulled even tighter. Posts had been set firmly in the ground and the ropes were wound round them, pegging Hotupuku firmly down until, at length, he lay lifeless, swathed with ropes and bleeding from a hundred wounds. His appearance was that of a huhu grub swollen to the size of a sperm whale.

One of the chiefs suggested that they all throw off their garments and cut the monster open in order that the contents of his belly might be inspected. The warriors set to using knives made of stone and obsidian, saws made of wood with triangular sharks' teeth set in them and sharp shells.

They had to cut through many layers of fat before they could open the belly. When the excited warriors had finally done this they exposed a grisly treasure trove. The first sight that met the horrified gaze of the beholders was a number of bodies of men, women and children that had recently been eaten and were still undigested. There were also separated limbs and torsos and heads. Also, it was found that the taniwha had swallowed everything that its victims were carrying.

There were greenstone mere, thrusting weapons such as kōkiri, taiaha and tewhatewha, whalebone weapons, darts and clubs, greenstone ornaments, sharks' teeth, mats, precious garments made of dogs' hair and those ornamented with albatross, kiwi and kākā feathers, garments of dressed and undressed flax and many other precious possessions.

The human remains were interred, after which the taniwha was butchered and the oil expressed from its fat. The taniwha was cooked and eaten by the warriors to celebrate their victory over the enemy that had killed their friends from Taupō-moana.

The Talking Taniwha of Mamaku

People travelling over the Mamaku Range between Waikato and Rotorua were forced to take a long detour to bypass a man-eating taniwha that lived in the mountains. The only man who used the direct route past the taniwha's lair was the Waikato chief Kahukiterangi, who was in love with Koka, the daughter of the old Te Arawa tohunga Pouwhenua.

Kahu was able to use the direct route because he had learnt from his father how to communicate with taniwha. His father had been a noted taniwha-killer and had learned their language through his many contacts with the strange, repulsive creatures.

Kahu knew that he could gain favour with Pouwhenua if he could make the direct route across the hills available once more to the Te Arawa people. He raised the matter with Pouwhenua on one of his visits but the tohunga could see no prospect of people using the path while the taniwha remained there.

Kahu flattered the old man. 'You are well able to subdue it by your magic arts,' he said. 'If you do that I will undertake to get my people to make a broad, smooth path through the hills and the forests.'

'And what is the condition of this generous offer?' the tohunga asked suspiciously.

'All I ask is that you let me have your daughter Koka as my wife.'

The tohunga pondered. He knew that such a marriage would strengthen the bonds between Te Arawa and Waikato peoples, while the path would the enable their toa to join forces against a common enemy. Therefore, despite still having some reservations, he accepted the proposal from Kahukiterangi.

On his return journey, Kahu climbed the hill and came to the taniwha's lair. He walked up to the taniwha and began to scratch and rub the beast's back, which is something that taniwha particularly like. In the hot afternoon sun the taniwha and the man talked together.

'You should have a wife,' Kahu said. 'A woman could look after you and massage your skin when it gets dry and itchy.'

'That is a fine idea,' the taniwha said. 'You may think it curious, but the same thought has occurred to me. Tell me, where do I find this wife? No one except you ever uses the track nowadays, because everyone knows of my presence.'

'I can get you a wife,' the wily Kahu said. 'But if I provide you with a woman, you must promise me one thing.'

'What is that?'

'That you will move to the other side of the mountain and leave the people of Waikato and Rotorua alone.'

'I would gladly do that,' the taniwha said. 'There is no purpose in remaining here where no food ever passes by.'

'Then I will bring you a wife in two days' time. See that you keep your part of the bargain.'

Kahu returned to his tribe and sought out an old woman named Pūkaka. She was repulsive in appearance and of a bitter disposition. She had been relegated to the task of burying the dead and was therefore shunned by her people.

'Pūkaka,' Kahu said, 'I have found a husband for you.'

The old woman pushed her matted hair to one side and looked at him sceptically. 'No one would willingly take me for a wife,' she muttered.

'Yes they would. Your husband is waiting eagerly for you now.'

'Where is he?'

'He is on the hill between here and Rotorua.'

'But the only living thing there is the taniwha.'

'Yes. It is the taniwha who will be your husband. He will provide for you and take care of you.'

The old woman was thoughtful. 'A husband for my old age,' she mused. 'Yes, the home of a taniwha is better than dying of starvation. I will go.'

Taking her filthy hand in his, Kahu led Pūkaka along the path until he came to the rua. The taniwha and the old woman regarded each other with mutual dislike, but eventually they decided to make the best of a poor bargain.

Kahu took leave of them. His last words to Pūkaka were, 'Remember to scratch his back when it becomes itchy and he will do anything you want. For your sake and for mine, see that he remains on the far side of the hill.'

As Kahukiterangi made his way down the track the taniwha lifted Pūkaka on to his back and, by magic, flew high into the air. He landed on the far slopes of the mountain to make a new home for himself and his bride.

With the menace removed the Waikato men set to work to stamp a trail through the undergrowth, cutting down trees that could not be avoided and using the branches to fill in the swampy patches. It was not long before Kahu and his friends were able to walk quickly and safely to Rotorua, where he was married to Koka. The marriage feast lasted many days and then the Waikato people returned to their homes accompanied by others from Rotorua, who were making a return visit. There were men, women and children in the long, straggling procession, including many young women who were the bride's friends and family.

No one spared a thought for the taniwha that had terrorised the travellers for so long. The laughter would have died in their throats if they had known that he was lying in a hollow a little distance above them, hidden by the tall tree-ferns. The taniwha was dissatisfied with his wife. From far away he had heard the shouts of laughter and the songs of the happy people. Curiosity had brought him over the hilltop to his present hiding place.

He was filled with a cold anger when he saw Kahu leading his beautiful bride along the track accompanied by a retinue of plump and attractive young women, while the skinny, dirty old burial woman of Waikato had been palmed off to him.

He surged out of the hollow and gathered two or three young women in one of his claws. Kahu heard the screams and came running back along the track to see what was happening. The taniwha swept over his head, paused to snatch Koka up with the other claw and sailed over the trees, back to his old rua on the crest of the hill.

When he returned home the broken-hearted Kahu consulted his father, asking how he could overcome the taniwha who had broken his promise. The plan they evolved between them was a good one and Kahu saw that every detail was attended to properly.

A few days later a band of young men left the pā and travelled swiftly until they came to the place where broken bushes and crushed grass indicated the route to the taniwha's cave. In an open space they stretched a thick flax rope in the form of a noose across the path. Part of the noose was held high in the air by means of a forked stick. The ends of the noose were carried through the long grass and into the forest, where they were grasped by a hundred hands on each side.

Kahu took off his garments and climbed the mountain slope alone. He made no attempt to disguise his approach. When he emerged in the open space in front of the cave he stood still for a moment, his heart beating quickly with apprehension. The blood-stained bones and fragments of flesh showed clearly that the taniwha had been feasting on the succulent young women of the two tribes.

Kahu shouted loudly, 'Come out, you cowardly monster, you treacherous creature.'

The taniwha's head appeared at the entrance to the cave. 'Oh, it is you, Kahu. Have you come to see my new wife, who is so plump and pretty, or would you rather have Pūkaka? She is waiting for you on the other side of the mountain. You may take her and then we will both be satisfied.'

'Where is Koka?' Kahu asked hoarsely.

'She is in the cave. She will make a fine mate for an old taniwha. Do not be alarmed, I am looking after her well.'

'I have come to take her away,' Kahu said coldly. 'Nothing can stop me. But first I will kill you and burn your vile body.'

The taniwha laughed. 'It would take an army of weaklings like you to

capture me. Unless you go quickly, I will come out and snap your spine and throw you as a tidbit for the kāhu and the kiore.'

Kahu made no reply to the threat but thrust out his tongue and made his eyes bulge in a defiant, insulting pūkana gesture. The taniwha sprang out of the cave and rushed at the young man, who turned and fled. Together they sped down the steep slope; Kahu, slim and naked, springing lightly down the path with the taniwha close behind him. The young man rushed through the noose, shouting, 'Now!' as he went.

One of his friends snatched the pole away as the taniwha drew level with it. The rope settled lightly round his neck, tightened then sank deeply into his flesh. The taniwha was arrested in mid-flight. The toa held on to the ropes, straining at them until the tightening noose strangled the faithless taniwha.

For the third time Kahukiterangi ascended the hill. He grasped his wife in his strong arms, comforting her before taking her down the hill and back along the newly made track to Waikato.

A Taniwha of Kaipara

One day three women from a kāinga to the south of Kaipara Harbour set out to gather a supply of tawa berries. One of them, younger than the others, was a beautiful young woman, while the other two were plain-looking. Their search took them a long distance from home. When they were finally satisfied with what they had gathered, they came unexpectedly on a wide path that they had never seen before. It appeared to be well used, which roused their curiosity.

They followed it for some distance until they came to a palisade overgrown with creepers. They tried to look through the gaps between the posts and as they did so they heard a roaring sound. The ground shook and a taniwha appeared. The women fled down the path, their berries scattering as they ran. The taniwha bounded along with huge strides and caught one of them. He looked at her face and threw her to one side, setting off in pursuit of the other two. On capturing the second woman he was again dissatisfied; but when he reached the third, who was young and good-looking, he picked her up and took her back to his cave.

Taniwha have the reputation of guarding their captives well and this one was no exception. The young woman had to resign herself to her unfortunate fate. As the years went by she bore sons to the taniwha. Three were monsters like their father, but the other three were normal babies who grew into strong young men. It was through her sons that the woman planned to make her escape and avenge herself on her monstrous husband.

As the taniwha continued to keep a jealous eye on her she educated all her children impartially. She taught the arts of weaving, cooking and domestic affairs to the monsters while to her natural sons she gave instruction in the arts of war, helping them to fashion weapons and training them in their use. The taniwha was satisfied, thinking that his family would be able to care for him in the home and bring food from the forest.

At last there came a day when he was absent from home. The woman called her children together and proposed an eel-catching expedition. They were all anxious to go, and so this ill-matched family set off. When they came to a clearing in the forest she sat down and told the human children to show their skill in attack and defence. When their blood was roused she said, 'Now attack your brothers!'

Without hesitation, for there had always been jealousy between the members of the family who were so different from each other, they set about them with mere and taiaha. The taniwha children were unable to defend themselves and before long the three of them were killed.

'It is a good deed you have done today,' the mother told her three boys. 'Now you know that you are men and belong to the tribe of my father. You are my sons! Will you free me from the taniwha who is your father?'

The boys were anxious to do so. They moved lightly and quickly through the forest and arrived at the dim cave. Their father had returned.

'Now!' whispered their mother excitedly.

They rushed inside and attacked the taniwha before he woke. In a few minutes the blood that flowed across the floor of the cave was a sign to their mother that the taniwha was dead and her years of suffering were avenged. To make doubly sure the boys cut off the limbs and left them lying in front of the cave.

After a long walk across the hills and through the forest, the mother and her three sons entered the kāinga where she had been born. She was recognised with tears and laughter, and that night there was great rejoicing. Even the old men of the tribe praised her sons for their valour and loyalty. But one old man got up and demanded attention.

'What have you done with the body of the taniwha?' he asked.

'We cut off his arms and legs and left them outside the cave,' they replied.

'And where is his body?'
'It is still lying inside the cave.'
'Is it big and fat?'
'Yes, it is very big and well conditioned.'
The old man looked at his people, who gazed at him attentively.
'I can smell cooked flesh,' he said. 'It is the flesh of the taniwha. It is rich and succulent.'

Everyone shouted in agreement. The next morning the hapū set out for the hills, led by the sons of the taniwha. There lay the limbs, with the body inside the cave, as they had described them. A huge oven was prepared, and the body and the limbs of the taniwha were put into it and covered over. Everyone waited until the cooking was completed. The earth and the mats were removed. To their horror the eyes of the taniwha rolled around and his body quivered and twitched. The limbs moved of their own accord and joined on to the body again.

The taniwha sprang out of the pit with steam rising from his sides and attacked the petrified onlookers. Many were killed where they stood, but some ran panic-stricken to escape from his gaping mouth and the death-dealing blows of his tail and limbs.

The taniwha ran after them. One woman ran to the top of a cliff by the sea and was thrown headlong into the water. It is said of her that the atua of the ocean saved her. They wrapped her in soft sponge and seaweed and rocked her in the waves, feeding her with seafood until finally she was cast ashore at Waiarohia. There the mass of seaweed was found by some fishermen. They cut it open and found the woman alive inside and returned her to her home.

There were friends there to meet her.

Not all the people had been killed when the taniwha came to life. Most of them had escaped. They had rallied together, crept up on him when he was resting and satiated with human food, and slew him a second time. On this occasion they took no risks. The body was cut into small pieces, the bones taken out, and the pieces of flesh burned separately to prevent them from coming together again, while fish-hooks and spear points were fashioned from the bones.

Te Kaiwhakaruaki

Two hundred travellers at a time were no more than a single meal for the gigantic Te Kaiwhakaruaki, which lived in the Parapara Stream, near Collingwood in Golden Bay. It preyed on travellers from Whakatū (Nelson), Tākaka and Motupipi who had to cross the Parapara Stream on their journey westwards.

It had the reputation of not allowing a single person to escape, no matter how large the party might be. It took the combined forces of the Ngāi Tahu, Ngāti Apa, Rangitāne, Ngāti Tūmatakōkiri, Ngāi Tara and Te Āti Awa tribes to vanquish the monster.

All attempts to subdue Te Kaiwhakaruaki had failed when a large party of Ngāi Tahu from Arahura, on the West Coast, travelled to Taitapu (Golden Bay) to visit the chiefs Pōtoru and Te Kohata. The visitors had heard reports of the monster and these were confirmed by Pōtoru.

Among the Ngāi Tahu visitors was a man who was famous as a killer of seals, noted for his ability to slay them with his bare hands. This man listened carefully to what Pōtoru had to say. He rose to his feet and said defiantly, 'Show me where this taniwha is and I will kill it with one blow of my fist.'

He sat down. Many of the listeners stared in astonishment at the boaster, but his own people were quick to explain that that was his method of killing seals.

Pōtoru replied: 'That will be your method, and we shall see what happens. If that doesn't work I have devised a plan to kill the monster.'

After further discussion it was decided that the seal hunter should be allowed to show his prowess, but that Pōtoru's plan should also be put into effect.

Three hundred and forty men were chosen. They felled a pōhutukawa, reputed to be the only one growing in the district, and made 340 weapons from its timber. Then they set out for the Parapara Stream.

When they were some distance away, Pōtoru halted them and told them his plan of attack.

'We shall divide into three parties,' he said. 'One hundred men will hide on the left of the track that leads to the stream and another hundred to the right. The main body will advance down the track and entice the taniwha on to land. When it rushes at them they will retire, and the flankers will open the attack from either side. When it swings its tail to the right, the men on the other side will advance; when it lunges to the left, the others will rush to the attack. In this way Te Kaiwhakaruaki will become tired and, if we are strong and unwearied, will fall to our blows.'

He stepped back and the seal hunter took his place.

'Listen, warriors! Have no fear of the taniwha. Think of it no more. I will go before you and enter the water and do battle with it. That is all.'

'It is well,' Pōtoru replied. 'Go forward and we will follow. If you fail we will put my plan into action.'

They came to the stream but there was no sign of Te Kaiwhakaruaki. The seal hunter entered the water.

'Be careful,' Pōtoru called to him. 'Do not let your bravery make you foolish. If the monster appears to be overcoming you, leave it to the warriors.'

'I will be careful,' the seal hunter replied. 'Remember that nothing has escaped my arm to this day.'

'Go!' said Pōtoru. 'Go! My ancestors say, "Go!"'

The lone hunter entered the water up to his waist and threw a basket of kōkōwai into the ngārara's lair. A huge wave of water rushed out of the cave, followed by the taniwha. The hunter retreated until the water was only up to his knees. The taniwha was close to him, its jaws open wide, when the hunter struck with all his might. His bare fist landed on the monster's snout and, such was the force of the blow, Te Kaiwhakaruaki's head was twisted to one side.

It bellowed with rage and rushed again at the intrepid hunter. Again his fist swung up, but the ngārara's mouth gaped even wider and the hunter was engulfed in it. The forward lunge that he had made carried him right into the monster's throat; the jaws clamped together and the man was lost to sight. As he disappeared, two of his friends who were standing on the bank cried, 'That is your house that you have entered.'

Te Kaiwhakaruaki pursued the pair as they fled up the track. Ahead of it were the massed ranks of the 140 men. It ran eagerly towards them, but as it passed the ambush the hidden warriors on either side of the track struck fiercely at its sides. Lashing and struggling from side to side it dug a hole two metres deep.

Pōtoru's plan was successful and the monster was destroyed. Its body was dismembered and its belly cut open to reveal the bodies and bones of many victims, and many treasures of wood, bone and greenstone. Whether the seal hunter escaped alive from his entombment in the belly of Te Kaiwhakaruaki we are not told.

SUPERNATURAL CREATURES, GIANTS AND FLYING MEN

It is not really very accurate to use terms taken from Western folklore, such as ogres, ogresses and giants, to label the monstrous and supernatural inhabitants of Aotearoa. In using these terms we need to bear in mind that these same creatures may also have been regarded as atua (gods), kaitiaki (guardians) and tūpuna (ancestors).

There are more tales of wicked female witches and ogresses in Māori tradition than there are of male ogres. There is something deeply disturbing in the idea of mothers and grandmothers, usually the nurturers within society, biting off children's heads and running people through with their fingernails. Often with the ogresses and witches their true nature is not immediately apparent, even to their husbands and children.

Many of the stories of witches and ogresses were told in the whare tapere at night, to the huge enjoyment of the listeners — though small children may well have clung to their mothers while the fitful flames caused dark shadows to leap and pounce around them.

Legends of men of giant stature vary from enormous beings who could move mountains or stride across Raukawa Moana (Cook Strait), to ancestors such as Tūhourangi, who was reputed to be nine feet in height. There was Kiharoa of Ngāti Raukawa and Ngāti Whakatere, who was said to be twice the height of an ordinary man. When he was defeated in battle, the oven prepared for his body was so large that the depression in the ground became known as the giant's grave.

Tūhourangi, who was six feet to his armpits and nine feet to the top of his head, had a voice that matched his size. When he shouted to his slaves from the shores of Rotorua he could be heard seven kilometres away at Mokoia Island. Tūhourangi was outmatched by Te Pūtē of Ngāpuhi, whose eyes were said to be as big as saucers and whose sneeze could be heard from Punakitere to Kaikohe, a distance of more than ten kilometres.

In Marlborough the Rapuwai, who preceded Kupe, were gigantic in size, but slow and clumsy. They were renowned fighters, crushing their enemies in their strong arms.

In Te Urewera, Te Ōtāne was so large that four men could stand inside his girdle and it took two men to carry his māipi (wooden weapon). Further north, at Whangaroa Harbour, there are still traces of the ancestor Tāwhaki. He ascended a natural rock ladder in the cliffs, then stepped from Māhinepua (Stephenson Island) to the mainland, and from one bay to another, in a single stride. On the rock beside Tāwhaki's track is a large red boulder where he stubbed his toe and the blood ran over the rock.

In Taranaki, Pāroa Reef bears tribute to the vast stature of a tohunga of Ngāti Tama. It is separated from the Taranaki Reef as though it had been severed by an adze. Ancient legend says that the rich, mussel-bearing reef was cut in two by this tohunga with the famous adze Poutamawhiria, and the Pāroa portion floated away to his own territory. The adze disapproved of being made a party to the theft and, as it bit into the reef, a corner of the blade broke off in protest. Many years later, when the traditional adze was rediscovered, the corner was found to be chipped, and this was interpreted as supporting the tradition.

Although we are not given any description of the famous fisherman Taramainuku, it may be presumed that he was a giant, for he cast his net across the Hauraki Gulf from Cape Colville to Whāngārei Heads. Taranga and Marotiri (Hen and Chickens Islands) and other islands were Ngā Pōitoo-te-kupenga-a-Taramainuku (The floats of Taramainuku's net), while Hauturu (Little Barrier Island) was the centrepost.

Taramainuku closely observed Moehau and Hauturu for signs that the wind would cease and the seas die down, so that he could put out his net. It was for this reason that he gave the names Moehau (Sleeping wind) and Hauturu (Resting post of the wind). The net itself was an extensive reef and it was believed that if a whale swam in it could not escape, but would eventually die in the gulf.

Kōpūwai
of the Matau

Kōpūwai (belly full of water) had the body of a man, the head of a dog and was covered with scales, like a fish. Like a dog, he had a keen sense of smell that was as effective on water as on land, and he himself had a pack of fierce, two-headed dogs. He lived in a cave near the present town of Cromwell, about a kilometre from the Matau (Clutha) River. The favourite prey of Kōpūwai and his dogs were men and women, and he ranged far and wide in search of food.

Near the mouth of the Matau there was a large pā occupied by a hapū of the Rapuwai tribe. In order to keep their whata well stocked during the cold winter months, the tribespeople foraged far and wide across the plain and up the river valley, catching fish and eels and hunting birds in the forests.

When some hunting expeditions failed to return, the people were distressed. At first they accepted the fact that there were always some losses due to accidents and encounters with enemy parties. However, as the number of hunting parties that failed to return grew, they became alarmed and began to take precautions.

One hunting group consisted of young women as well as men. One of the women, whose name was Kaiamio, became separated from the others. Kōpūwai had been lurking in the bush observing the hunters. When he saw that Kaiamio had been left so far behind that her cries could no longer be heard, he unleashed his two-headed dogs, which ran around her, barking savagely. Kaiamio shrank back, but her terror increased tenfold when she saw the dog-like face of the monster and felt his scaly arms lifting her from the ground. Kōpūwai moved swiftly, carrying the girl up to his cave where she was guarded by a ring of snarling dogs.

Kaiamio had no doubt about what would happen to her. Tales of Kōpūwai's human feasts had recently been told in the pā.

However, a different fate was in store for her. The girl was so beautiful that Kōpūwai's cold heart was touched. He determined to keep her as a wife, but he had no intention of pampering her. She soon learned that she was to cook for him and generally look after his needs.

He would not trust her outside the cave; when he went to the river to fetch water he tied a long flax rope to her hair. He kept one end of the rope in his hand and tugged it from time to time to make sure she was in the cave. His vigilance never relaxed. The years passed and Kaiamio remained in loathsome captivity. Her people had searched for her, but Kōpūwai's cave was well hidden and she had long been given up for dead.

Kaiamio never lost hope of escaping. When the time came and she was allowed to go to the river and draw water, Kōpūwai still took the precaution of tying a rope to her hair. For months she snatched a few moments each time she was at the water's edge to gather kōrari (flax stalks) and tie them in bundles with strips of flax leaves. The bundles were laid side by side and tied firmly together until at last she had a mōkihi (raft of flax stalks), which would bear her weight on the river.

One morning she left the cave early. Reaching the riverbank she took the rope from her hair and tied it to the root of a clump of raupō. She launched the mōkihi hastily and was soon speeding down the river, looking fearfully behind her lest Kōpūwai and his vile dogs should appear on the bank in pursuit. The monster had been lying asleep in the hot sun, waking every now and then to tug the rope, which gave gently and assured him that his wife was still secure.

After a while a seed of doubt was sown in his mind. There was no slack, which seemed to indicate that she had stayed in one place for a long time. Calling his dogs to him, Kōpūwai hurried down to the river. When he saw that the rope was tied to some raupō and that there was no sign of Kaiamio, he realised that he had been tricked. Howling with rage, he sent his dogs questing along the bank. When they returned he knew that his wife must have escaped down the river. He plunged his head into the water and drank until the river was dry, but fresh inflow from the lake filled the riverbed again and the monster returned home in disgust.

Kaiamio's appearance at the pā was greeted with cries of incredulity and delight. At night the people of the pā wept with her and listened with horror to the story of her imprisonment. They resolved to eliminate the man-eating monster of the hills now that Kaiamio could guide them to his lair. She told them that it would be better to wait for the summer before setting out, because when the warm north-west wind blew Kōpūwai grew sleepy and he could easily be overcome by armed men.

Some months later a strong expedition set off for the monster's cave. The men gathered dry raupō and kōrari as they went. When they drew near to the cave, Kaiamio was sent ahead to reconnoitre. She returned and said that the time was favourable. She had seen Kōpūwai and his dogs fast asleep inside the cave. The fighting men crept forward and piled the dry vegetation in front of the entrance. There was a hole in the roof of the cave and the boldest warriors stationed themselves there.

A torch was thrust into the heap of dry grass, flax stalks and wood. The fire crackled through it and the wind carried the flames into the dark interior of the cave. The smoke choked the barking of the dogs, though two of them sprang through the wall of flame and made their escape. As for Kōpūwai, he tried to climb through the vent in the roof, but as soon as his dog-like head appeared, he was battered to death by the waiting warriors.

The original name for the Old Man Range is Kōpūwai, named after the monster whose body was represented by a huge pillar of stone on the summit of the range. The dogs that escaped fled to another cave at present-day Duntroon, where they were turned to stone, and could afterwards be seen with their forepaws hanging out of the cave. Some of the dogs were said to lie beneath the surface of a pool in the Ōtakaroa Stream, which was used by the local people as a mirror for grooming their hair.

Houmea and Uta

Houmea lived long ago and was an ancestress of the famous Paikea. She was married to Uta and they had two children, Tūtawhake and Nini.

On one occasion Uta went fishing. He spent a long day in his canoe and caught many fish. When he returned it was evening. He waited for Houmea to come down to the beach to carry the fish up to their home. When some time had passed and she had not arrived, he went up the path to the whare and shouted, 'Mother, Mother! There was I on the beach, waiting for a long time, but you did not come.'

'Husband!' she replied. 'The reason for my not coming was the disobedience of our children.'

Uta went inside, while Houmea ran down to the beach. When she got to the canoe she lifted out the fish, but instead of carrying them up to her home, she swallowed them whole. There were many fish in the canoe, but by the time Houmea had finished, there was not one left.

Naturally she wished to disguise her greed from her husband. She trampled in the soft sand and pulled up small bushes by the roots, dragging them backwards and forwards to give the impression that many people had been there. Then she rushed up the path and flung herself through the door, panting for breath.

'Auē, Uta! There were no fish in your canoe. A party of our enemies has raided it and taken them all.'

Uta sprang to his feet. 'What nonsense is this? Who would dare to come so close to my home?'

'You must see for yourself. Many people have been there.'

Uta was angry. 'Again, I say nonsense! No warrior would dare to steal from the gateway of my kāinga. You must be mistaken, woman.'

'I am not mistaken, because the fish are gone and I have seen footprints in the sand. If it was not men who came, it might well have been Te Tini-o-Te-Hakuturi.'

Te Tini-o-Te-Hakuturi was the tribe of forest guardians including birds and insects who intervened in human affairs from time to time when people did not follow proper protocols.

The following day Uta took his canoe to sea and caught many more fish. In the late afternoon he beached his canoe and waited for his wife. When she did not come, he went up to the whare and reproached her again.

'Mother, Mother! Am I to remain forever on the sand? I have been waiting for you there and you did not come. Indeed, you have done nothing to help me.'

Houmea went down to the beach and devoured the fish again; but Uta's suspicions had been roused. He sent his children to watch her. They hid in the bushes and saw everything she did. As soon as Houmea had eaten the catch, Tūtawhake and Nini ran back to their father and told him what they had seen.

'Father, Father! It was our mother who swallowed all the fish!'

Uta waited until his wife returned and listened patiently to her tale of marauders who had taken the fish while the canoe was left unattended. Then he said quietly: 'Wife, where are the men of whom you speak? Can you show them to me? Let me tell you that our children were there and they saw you — and no one but you — swallowing the fish I have caught today.'

Houmea was covered with shame, but she blustered and held to her story. She protested that she had been a model wife and had never committed any crime, either of adultery or theft. Uta said nothing, until she faltered in her speech and had no more words to offer. He turned his back on her and retired to his sleeping mat; but Houmea's heart was dark and she vowed vengeance on the children who had betrayed her.

When Uta next went fishing, Houmea took advantage of her opportunity. She sent Nini to fetch water from the spring. When she was alone with Tūtawhake, she told him to lie down in order that she might remove the lice from his hair. As he squatted down she opened her mouth and swallowed him. When Nini returned with the water, she swallowed her too.

Uta came up the path. Before he reached his home he heard Houmea groaning. The whare was filled with blowflies, many of which had settled on her face and lips.

'Mother dear, are you ill?' he asked.

'Yes, I am ill.'

'Whereabouts is the atua that is gnawing at you?'

'In my stomach and bowels.'

There was nothing that Uta could do to help her. Then he asked, 'Where are my children?'

Houmea's head rolled helplessly on her shoulders.

'I do not know. I have not seen them for some time. When I became ill they ran away. How can I possibly know where they are?'

There was something evasive in her tone. Uta bent over to examine her more closely, and noticed blood on her lips and her swollen stomach. With fear in his heart, he repeated an incantation:

Attack, strike on end, hit away upwards,
Turn it, ward it off on one side.
Make the food swallowed by the great kawau come out.
Let it be open, let it be clear.
The obstruction is cleared away by the karakia,
The obstruction is caught in a noose of flax and carried off,
The obstruction that confines Tūtawhake.

As the karakia was concluded Houmea's mouth gaped wide, her stomach convulsed and her children were regurgitated, alive and well. Tūtawhake carried a taiaha and Nini a huata (spear) and they ran to their father, who wept over them.

After this Uta realised that his wife was an ogress and that neither he nor his children were safe from her. He called Tūtawhake and Nini to him and told them to pay close attention to him.

'This is my word to you both. When I ask you to fetch me some water, refuse to do it. Then I shall pretend to be angry and I will threaten you with a stick, but take no notice. You may have to hide, but whatever you do, do not on any account go to the spring to get water. Do you understand what I say?'

The children looked puzzled, but said they would do as their father instructed. Sometime later, when the family was gathered together, Uta ordered them to fetch water from the spring. They refused point-blank; no matter how much he shouted, they grew more and more stubborn.

Uta turned to his wife and said, 'Mother dear, will you fetch me some water to drink? I am dying of thirst, and these ungrateful children will not obey me.'

Houmea took the calabash and went to the spring; but no sooner had she left the whare than Uta began another incantation:

> Let the water sink into the earth,
> Let the water be decreased,
> Let the water dry up,
> Go on, Hou, go on,
> Away, away, to the source of the stream,
> To the distant hills.

The words of the incantation were fulfilled. As Houmea approached, the stream dried up and the water retreated. She followed it swiftly, but the dry stones in the bed of the creek mocked her. As soon as she was out of sight, Uta took his children down to the canoe. They carried the embers of the household fire with them and set them on a fireplace of stones on the decking.

Uta turned back and commanded the structures and physical features in and around his village to answer Houmea's questions when she returned. By gestures he indicated the whare and the palisades of the village, the trees, the latrine and the brow of the hill, including them all in his commands.

Then he and the children embarked on the canoe, unfurled the sail and put out to sea.

When Houmea returned she went straight to the whare, infuriated that her search had been in vain. She could not understand why there was no reply to her complaints, until she looked inside and found there was no one there. She went outside and called to them, but was bewildered by the echoes.

'Where are you?' she cried, and echoes from the whare, palisades, latrine, trees and hills all answered, 'Where are you? Are you? You?'

Houmea felt faint with disappointment and frustration. She looked across the sea. Away in the distance she could discern a speck on the horizon that she knew must be the canoe bearing her husband and children away from her. She ran down the path to the beach and along a sandy spit, where she changed into a kawau (shag) and floated out on the ebbing tide.

Tūtawhake and Nini kept looking back as the canoe sailed before the wind. Soon they saw the kawau swimming towards them so rapidly that they knew it would soon catch them. They knew that it was their mother and they turned to Uta in a frenzy.

'Father, the atua is coming after us!'

Uta was asleep, but he woke quickly, infected by their panic.

'Oh, my children, what shall we do? We will be swallowed up by her, for she is a demon. We will be engulfed in her stomach!'

His dependence on them brought fortitude to the children.

'Do not be afraid, Father,' they said. 'We will hide you beneath the floorboards. She will never find you there.'

Houmea reached the canoe. Holding on to the side, she changed back into her own form, so that Tūtawhake and Nini, peering down, were able to see down her huge throat into her dark, cavernous belly.

'Where is my food?' she demanded.

'It is not here,' the children said. 'It is still at home, far behind us. Go back and you will see that there are plenty of fish left in the village.'

'Why have you come so far out from the land?'

'We came to catch more fish, but the wind has blown us offshore.'

Houmea tightened her grip. The canoe tipped and the waves splashed over the strakes.

'I am nearly dead of starvation,' she croaked.

The children took fish that had been roasting in the fireplace and threw them down her throat.

'More, more!' she cried. 'You must have plenty of fish. Give me more.'

'Be patient!' Tūtawhake reproved her. He turned back to the fire and, using two sticks, removed one of the stones, which by this time was red hot. Then he shouted to his mother, 'Open your mouth wide. Here is a tasty morsel.'

As Houmea's mouth split even further apart, he thrust the large stone into it. The ogress closed her jaws and swallowed the stone. For a moment there was a horrible smell of burning and a hiss of boiling liquid. The ogress released her hold on the canoe and sank swiftly down through the water. A huge bubble rose to the surface, there was a smell of decay in the air and a patch of oil circled the spot where she had disappeared.

Although that was the end of Houmea, the kawau is a constant reminder of her and her name is applied to evil women to this day.

Te Ngārarahuarau

Te Rorongia-rahia was a young woman whose beauty and modesty were such that her fame had spread to the surrounding tribes, even as far as the distant kāinga where Ruruteina and his brothers lived. Ruru was the youngest of the family and, as so often happens to the last-born, his elder brothers assigned the meanest tasks to him and thought him little better than a slave. The young men had heard so much of Te Rorongia that they decided to pay her a visit to see if they could win her as a wife. There was some jealousy between them, but Ruru was not considered as a competitor. He was taken with them in order to cook their food on the journey.

They travelled by canoe. When they reached Te Rorongia's village they hurried ashore, leaving Ruru to carry their gifts and other belongings to the guest house where they were to stay. While Ruru was engaged in this task, his brothers went to the whare tapere where they settled themselves comfortably in anticipation of the evening's entertainment.

No one pointed out the famous Te Rorongia-rahia to them and their questions were deftly parried. Each brother therefore chose a girl of good appearance in the hope that she might turn out to be Te Rorongia. They remained by the side of the young women they had selected and during the evening each asked his companion her name.

The eldest brother was delighted when his companion whispered coyly, 'Do not tell anyone. I am Te Rorongia-rahia.' In low tones he declared his love and, to his great joy, the young woman consented to become his wife. She warned him that her parents would be angry and would not permit a betrothal. If he were to win her, he must carry her away secretly, hiding her in the canoe when he took his departure.

The first-born could hardly conceal his excitement. He looked pityingly at his brothers, each of whom seemed contented with the young woman of his choice. But he would have felt less satisfied if he had known that each of the young women accompanying his brothers also claimed to be Te Rorongia-rahia.

The puhi herself maintained her reputation for modesty. She had not entered the house of entertainment, nor seen the visitors. She remained quietly in her own whare and had no contact with the strangers.

While his brothers sat in the whare tapere courting, Ruruteina had been busily occupied in transporting supplies from the canoe to the guest house. When he had finished he went to replenish the water supply. No one had told him where the spring was to be found, so he asked some children to show him the way.

'There,' they said. 'That is the path. The spring is next to the whare of Te Rorongia-rahia.'

Ruru concealed his satisfaction at this news. When night fell and his brothers were occupied with the girls who were each pretending to be Te Rorongia-rahia, Ruru stole up to the whare. Te Rorongia-rahia was standing in the doorway. When she saw him her face lit up, for she had noticed him at his work during the afternoon. She greeted him courteously and invited him inside.

Ruru realised that this was a signal of favour and as he spoke with her, his heart went out to her. Long before the night's entertainment was over, they had declared their love. Ruru felt as though he was walking on air as he tiptoed back to the guest house. When his brothers came in later, they assumed that he had been asleep the whole time.

The brothers remained at the village for several days and each secretly congratulated himself on having captured the heart of the inaccessible Te Rorongia. On the night before their departure, Ruru and Te Rorongia knew that they could not bear to be parted again. While his brothers enjoyed the society of the young people in the whare tapere, Ruru led his betrothed down to the canoe and hid her securely. As befitted her position, she was accompanied by a female attendant.

At dawn the brothers came down to the canoe accompanied by the young women who had been entertaining them. Each of the brothers still believed that the girl of his choice was Te Rorongia-rahia, but had kept the secret to himself and prided himself on his conquest. The sail was set and the canoe glided away with its complement of young men and women.

After proceeding some distance there was a change in the wind and they were forced to take shelter in a small bay. The wind was cold and they went ashore to try and kindle a fire, but the wood was wet and would not burn. A plume of smoke was seen at a distance and Ruru was sent to investigate and, if possible, to bring back some fire. He was reluctant to go, fearing that Te Rorongia might be discovered during his absence, but his brothers would not accept his excuses and forced him to go.

When Ruru arrived at the place where the smoke had been seen, he found a large whare. Ruru met the female slaves Kioretī and Kioretā, who told him that the name of their mistress was Te Ngārarahuarau. The old woman called them inside and asked them whom they had been talking to.

'His name is Ruruteina,' they said.

'What is he doing here?'

'He has come to ask for some embers from the fire.'

The old woman nodded. 'Tell him to stay for a while and share our meal,' she ordered.

Ruru stayed, but when the meal was served he regretted it because, as her name implies (ngārara meaning reptile), Te Ngārarahuarau was half-woman and half-lizard. Her tail trailed behind her as she walked. She dragged it over Ruru and across the food, leaving a smear of filthy scales over everything.

When the meal was finished, Te Ngārarahuarau left. Ruru turned to the slaves and asked, 'Is she always like this?'

'Yes, always.'

'Is she a human being?'

'No, she is really a monster.'

Their conversation was interrupted by a shrill scream. Te Ngārarahuarau had overheard them. She shrieked, 'I will kill you.'

'Quick!' whispered Kioretī and Kioretā. 'Run away. If you don't go now you will never escape her.'

So they hid among the rocks while Ruru ran for his life, with Te Ngārarahuarau at his heels.

'Come back, Ruru, come back!' she cried.

The young man ran more swiftly than his pursuer. When she saw that he was escaping, she stopped and called, 'You may not see me on a fine day, but when a misty day comes, I will be with you.'

Trembling with fear and exhaustion, Ruru returned to his brothers and told them what had happened. 'I am afraid that she will find us. If she does, we will all be killed.'

His brothers agreed that the only way to rid themselves of the danger was to kill her. Working feverishly they built a tiny whare of raupō, with a door in front and a small window at the back. In the middle of the house they planted a heavy post and dressed it up in Ruru's cloak.

They waited for several days for the ogress to appear. At last there came a day when the mists crept down the flanks of the mountains and along the valleys until it reached the shore. The brothers were not far away from the tiny little whare they had built. Ruruteina was inside, hiding behind the post, when a voice was heard from the mist saying, 'Ruru, where are you?'

'Here,' he answered.

Te Ngārarahuarau thrust the door violently aside and went in. She saw the post dressed in Ruru's cloak and mistook it for the young man. She embraced it and wound her tail closely around it. While she clung to the dressed post, Ruru's brothers began to heap firewood and large branches against the walls.

'What is that noise?' Te Ngārara asked.

From behind the post Ruru answered, 'Don't take any notice. My brothers are preparing a meal for us.'

The young men put a torch to the firewood. As the first wisps of smoke drifted through the window, Ruru dived through it and made his escape.

The smoke swirled through the house, which broke into a mass of flame. Te Ngārara felt the searing heat and cried in agony, 'Ruru, you are forgetting me.'

She rushed to the door, but was driven back by the flames. She went to the window, but it was too small for her bulk. The walls were now blazing from top to bottom. The lizard ogress was doomed, but in her last extremity the scales of her skin tried to escape. The scales leapt out of the window and the holes that the fire had made in the walls, but Ruru and his brothers gathered round and struck at them with sticks and drove them back.

Only two of the scales managed to escape, turning into small lizards. When the fire died down there was nothing left of Te Ngārarahuarau.

With the menace removed from their lives the young men continued their journey and arrived at their home. The eldest son proudly led his young woman to his parents and introduced her as his wife, the famous Te Rorongia-rahia. His mother greeted her coldly, thinking that the virgin had been greatly overrated.

Her eyes widened as her second son came before her with another bold-eyed young woman, who also laid claim to being Te Rorongia-rahia. One after another, her sons introduced their wives as Te Rorongia-rahia. Their mother greeted each one coldly and politely and invited her to sit on the marae. When the last of them had been seated, she addressed her youngest son.

'What about you, Ruruteina? Are you the only one who has come back without a wife?'

Ruru smiled. 'Have you looked in the cabin of the canoe?' he asked.

'No. Why should we have occasion to look inside?'

'Please, my mother, do me that one favour. Go down to the canoe and see what is in the cabin.'

His mother went to the canoe and looked inside. There sat a girl to whom her heart warmed at once. The tears were running down Te Rorongia-rahia's face. A cooked pigeon that Ruru had smuggled into the canoe lay in front of her, barely tasted.

There was no need for Ruru's mother to be told who the young woman was. She rushed back to her people and called to them excitedly, 'Te Rorongia-rahia is in the canoe! It is she — the wife of our youngest son, who will be the pride of our kāinga and the comfort of our old age! Come and see!' When they realised they had been tricked, the other brothers beat their wives.

Te Ruahine-mata-māori

Although many of the witches and ogresses of legend are noted for their repulsive appearance, Te Ruahine-mata-māori was an exception. Her name means 'the old woman with the normal face'. Despite this she was not able to deceive the explorer Paowa, who immediately recognised Te Ruahine for what she was.

Travelling by canoe, Paowa and his men reached a distant shore and landed. He was greeted by Te Ruahine-mata-māori and invited to partake of a meal. She took a basket of small kūmara from her storehouse and placed them in the oven.

While they were cooking, Paowa asked if he could have a drink of water. Te Ruahine went to fetch some. As she left, Paowa bewitched the spring, causing it to dry up, or at least to appear to her to be dry. She went to another place, but found that that pool was empty too. Wherever she went, over the hills and valleys, she found that all the usual sources of water were dried up.

At length she realised that Paowa had seen through her pretence of hospitality and had recognised that she intended harm to him and his men. She looked back at her house and saw a tall column of smoke rising, but there was no sign of Paowa until she looked across the sea and saw his canoe dwindling into the distance.

She sang a mournful lament:

Kia wera rā taku whare,
Ko taku whata ka waiho.
Kia wera rā taku taumatua,
Ko taku rua ka waiho.
Kia wera rā taku māra,
Ko aku takitaki ka waiho.
Kia wera rā aku paepae tūtae,
Ko aku kurī ka waiho.

If my house is burnt,
Let my storehouse be spared.
If my ceremonial place is burnt,
Let my storage pit be spared.
If my cultivations are burnt,
Let my fences be spared.
If my latrines are burnt,
Let my dogs be spared.

Although Paowa's canoe was out of sight from land by now, the ogress was not to be so easily outdone. Te Ruahine called her dogs to her and asked them where her enemy had gone. They followed the man-scent down to the water's edge and sniffed among the seaweed. Then they pointed their noses to the horizon.

Te Ruahine placed some kura under her armpits, threw off her cloak and waded into the sea. The power of the sacred red kura enabled her to swim underwater quickly. After she had travelled many leagues in this fashion, she came to the surface and looked around. There was the canoe, not far away, close to a strange land. She swam underwater again and came up close to the canoe. Paowa had been watching and when he saw her head and shoulders rising above the waves, he urged his crew to paddle quickly to the shore.

The canoe surged ahead, but Te Ruahine-mata-māori drove through the waves like a war canoe, her breasts cleaving a passage through the water and her arms and legs thrashing like the flukes of a whale. As she reached out her hand to grasp the side of the canoe, Paowa shouted a last command to his men to paddle for their lives, then he jumped overboard. The canoe pulled away as Te Ruahine turned to chase her enemy.

He reached the shore ahead of her, ran up the beach and took refuge in a cave, frantically piling boulders across the entrance as the ogress rushed across the sand. By the time she came to the cave the barricade was firmly in position. She scratched at it vainly for a short while and then sat down in front of it.

Inside the cave Paowa kindled a fire and roasted some food he had with him. When he was ready he called to Te Ruahine-mata-māori, 'Old woman, where are you?'

'I am here,' she replied.

'Here is some food for you.'

He pushed it between the stones of the wall he had made and she snatched it up and ate it.

'Well, my grandson, that was a nice morsel.'

'I will give you some more. Shut your eyes and open your mouth.'

When her eyes were closed, Paowa used some sticks to thrust a red-hot stone from the cooking fire into her mouth. Te Ruahine swallowed it and fell to the ground. Paowa came out of the cave and bent over her. She was dead, but as soon as he touched her, lightning flashed from her armpits. He knew by this where she had hidden the kura.

With the sacred red ochre in his possession he was capable of miraculous deeds. As his men had departed in the canoe, he rolled a hollow log of wood down to the water and crawled inside it. By the power of the kura the log was propelled back to his home.

By this time his men had already returned and had spread the story that their leader had been killed by Te Ruahine. Preparations were already underway for a tangi. Food was being taken from the whata and hunting, eeling and fishing parties had been dispatched to bring in birds and fish for the ovens. Others were gathering firewood, including a group collecting driftwood who found Paowa's log washed up on the beach. They tried to lift it but it was too heavy, so they left it and carried the smaller pieces back to the kāinga.

When they had gone Paowa crawled out of the log. He hid his kura

away carefully. Disguising himself as an old man, he entered the village and accosted some women who were carrying the first baskets of food to the mourners.

'Give me something to eat,' he asked them.

One of the women looked scornfully at the old man.

'You are a bold person to ask for food that has been specially prepared for those who mourn for our rangatira Paowa.'

Another woman felt sorry for him. 'The poor old man!' she exclaimed. 'Give him something to eat.'

Some of the more kind-hearted women gave him a few dried fish.

Paowa said, 'Give me some oil.'

'No,' one of the women said sharply. 'It is only for mourners.'

But others said: 'There is plenty of it. We might as well give him some.'

Paowa took the oil. 'Now give me some clothes.'

Again some of the women objected, but others provided a kākahu kura (cloak covered with red feathers).

'But I am not properly dressed yet. I want some feathers for my hair.'

At this there was a chorus of protest, but the well-disposed women gave him some prized huia feathers. Paowa went down to the stream where he could see his reflection in the water and dressed himself carefully. He mixed the kura with oil and anointed his face and body until the moko stood out clearly. He put on the kākahu kura and threaded the huia feathers into his topknot.

Then he strode on to the marae with the air of an ariki, his cloak swinging, drawing exclamations of admiration from the onlookers. The magic power of the kura proved an effective disguise and no one recognised him.

The middle-aged women coveted him as a son-in-law. His every movement was observed. Paowa looked round him and recognised one of the women who had been so solicitous of his welfare. Her granddaughter was seated by her side. Paowa spoke fair words to the granddaughter and, as she responded modestly, he asked her to be his wife, to the great content of both the young woman and her grandmother.

The people gathered around and asked him who he was. Invoking the power of the kura, he instantly became recognisable and was greeted with cries of incredulity and pleasure. The feast of mourning was transformed into an occasion of joy. And there was not one at the feast who was more delighted than the old lady who had shown kindness to a stranger.

The Wives of Kametara

By his first wife Kametara fathered two children, a boy named Te Ngohi and a girl, Meranei. Sometime after their birth a strange woman came to the pā. She exercised an evil influence over Kametara, who took her as a second wife.

The two wives had no liking for each other. The aversion that the first wife had for the second was instinctive, for she had no idea that her rival was in fact a black-hearted ogress.

When Kametara went fishing his ogress wife waited for his return. Like a dutiful wife she gathered the fish out of the canoe and returned with them to the pā, but on the way she ate most of the catch just as it was, raw and unscaled.

After some time the first wife conceived again. The second wife was jealous and made a plan to get rid of her rival.

'Have you noticed how few fish our husband catches nowadays?' she enquired artfully.

'Yes, there seem to be very few of them when you bring them home.'

'I think our husband would be pleased if we tried to make ourselves useful. Let us take out a small canoe and see what we can do for ourselves.'

When the tiny canoe was out of sight of land, the ogress dropped the anchor and the two women began to fish. By her magic arts the ogress closed the mouths of the fish so that they could not bite. After waiting for a while the ogress suggested that they try somewhere else. Again using her magic powers, she caused the anchor stone to remain firmly on the seabed. All their efforts could not dislodge it.

'Dive down and see if you can find what is holding it,' the ogress said.

'No, it is too far down. Let us cut the rope.'

'We ought not to do that. It is Kametara's favourite anchor stone and he will be angry if we lose it.'

'But I cannot dive. My child lies heavy in my womb.'

'You must. It is your responsibility.'

After some further argument the first wife lowered herself over the side of the canoe and pulled herself down by the anchor rope. The ogress gave her time to reach the bottom and then cut the rope, snatched up her paddle and sent the canoe skimming towards the shore with powerful strokes.

The first wife felt the rope snaking downwards through the water. With lungs nearly bursting she rose to the surface and saw the canoe dwindling into the distance. She knew then that the ogress was her enemy and had left her to die. But she was a woman of spirit. Treading water, she chanted a karakia. The atua of the sea heard her prayer and sent a taniwha, who lifted her on his back and carried her safely to land. She had arrived at a distant, uninhabited part of the island.

She realised that if she returned to her home, the ogress would find some other way of getting rid of her. She could no longer trust her husband to defend her. Her first concern was for her immediate needs. She gathered fern root, the soft pith of tree ferns, wild turnips and pāua, and managed to kindle a fire. Her hunger satisfied, she made a temporary shelter and went to sleep.

The following morning she began to make preparations for a permanent home. In the course of time she gave birth to twin boys and, for some years, every moment was occupied in caring for them, gathering and cooking food and weaving garments.

As the boys grew older they were able to help their mother. She taught them how to make spears and snares to catch birds, and how to preserve the birds in their own fat. The boys found kūmara tubers that had been washed ashore. They took them to their mother, asking what they were. Her heart lightened when she saw the familiar vegetables. She urged them to search for more, planted them, and soon they were able to harvest a good crop each year.

In her spare time their mother had carved a wooden flute with three holes. She composed a song of love for her husband and her people and taught it to the boys. When they had learned it off by heart she told them to fell a tōtara tree and make a canoe. However, after a suitable tree had been felled, the boys had the same trouble with Te Tini-o-Te-Hakuturi as the famed Rātā — the forest guardians restored the tree each time they cut it down. Eventually they fought the forest folk and overcame them.

When the canoe was finished, their mother brought them piles of muka (dressed flax) and showed them how to make fishing lines and nets. They were sent fishing, the catch was dried in the sun and put in the storehouses.

Great piles of food had now been stored and the weather was calm. The mother called her sons to her.

'The time has come for you to visit my people. Take the canoe and follow the coast,' she said.

'When you come to the mouth of a river where mānuka grows thickly, go ashore and hide the canoe. Find the large whata that stands in the pā. Wait until it is dark and then go to the whata and sleep in it. As soon as it is light you must get up. One of you is to play the flute while the other sings the song I have taught you.

'If no one hears you, go to your sister Meranei's cooking-house and wait there. When she comes to prepare food she will see you.'

The young men set off in the canoe and followed all of their mother's instructions. They found the pā and slept in the whata. The following morning they sang their song:

> E rere, e te ao, e kume i runga rā,
> He iti taku ngākau, rahi atu i a au.
> Ka matua i a au te uri o Kametara;
> Ki a Arawiwī te pānga ki roto rā.
> Whakatau rawa iho te pēhi a Kupe,
> E Te Ngohitūpiki rāua ko Meranei,
> Ko Kametara te tau kia aropiri mai.
> Mā wai e whakaeke tō tau, e whae?

Aea ka ora me ko Ware — e.
Ka kai te titiro, ka ripa i a au.
Ki te whe-perohuka
Kei tata, e tukua te manako ki te iwi — e — i.

Fly, O mist! Draw along above,
Small though my heart is, it is greater than me.
I am the parent of Kametara's children;
Through love of Arawiwī is the anguish within me.
Weighed down am I by Kupe's ballast,
The separation from Te Ngohitūpiki and Meranei;
Kametara is the lover I would were near.
Who, O woman, will approach thy lover now?
Perchance it had been better were Ware there.
Now feeds the gaze, in vain thou art
Separated from me by the wide ocean.
Would I were near to express my love for my people.

The song ended and they sat still and listened. There was no sound or
movement in the pā. They played and sang again but still there was no
response. They crept out of the whata, found a cooking shelter that they
thought might be their sister's, went inside and covered themselves with
mats.

Presently Meranei came into the shelter. She looked at the mats lying
on the floor and cried, 'Oh, there are some men here!' She ran back to the
wharepuni and roused the others.

'There are two men in the cooking shelter!'

'Bring them here,' the people cried.

The young men were brought into the house.

'Who are you?' they were asked.

They told them who their mother was and where they lived and they
sang their song, which so delighted the people that they all learned to sing
it. Men and women rose to greet the young men and wept over them and
welcomed them into their midst.

'Auē! It is a great loss that Kametara and his second wife are not here

today,' they said. 'How proud Kametara would be of these two men who are like warriors!'

But Kametara and his ogress wife had gone away. After some days the people decided to visit the woman who had been the wife of their chief. The strakes were lashed to the canoes and the flotilla set sail.

The young men went first to warn their mother.

'Your children and all your people are coming,' they told her.

Her face lit up with joy. 'Let us prepare food for them,' she said.

By the time the food was cooked, the canoes had come into view. The mother and her sons put on their finest garments, the mother donning a parawai, a very fine flax cloak. She wept over her daughter Meranei and her eldest son, Te Ngohi, and all her relatives. The weeping, the laughter, the feasting and the giving of presents went on until all the stars came out and the moon shone on the scene of rejoicing.

It was a happy night and the happiness went on from day to day, and year to year, for the people had found it a well-favoured land. They went back to their pā and brought all their possessions with them and settled in the kāinga that their daughter and her sons had made.

Of Kametara and his ogress wife nothing more is heard. Perhaps they came back to find the weka and the kiwi and the kiore as the only inhabitants of their pā.

Toaangina

The scourge of the mouth of the Waikato River was Toaangina, a chief
who was so tall and strong that he might well be called a giant. He towered
head and shoulders above other warriors. Near his pā at Tauranganui he
tied a long vine to a tree-top and swung himself far over the water, where
he could see canoes travelling up and down the river. He could also see
men and women on the banks or in the water gathering shellfish. After
observing them in this way, he would creep through the bush and capture
or kill them.

He was most feared by those that travelled by canoe. If the voyagers
were foolhardy or careless enough to paddle past his village, Toaangina
would swing out on the vine and snatch a man out of the canoe with
one hand, while he held on to the vine with the other. The rope would
swing back to the bank with its double burden and his mere would claim
another victim. Sometimes he would seize the canoe and drag it to the
shore. Even if the canoe hugged the far bank, it would not be safe from the
giant chief. Toaangina would put out in his own canoe, propelling it with
strong strokes that sent the smooth water curling past the sides, until he
had overtaken his victims. He would then throw a noose over the stern-
piece of the canoe and tow it back to his pā, where the crew would be
imprisoned and devoured at Toaangina's pleasure.

Naturally some measures were taken to remove the menace, but such
was his strength and overwhelming size that the chief was able to defeat
all his enemies. One of the most indignant chiefs was Korongoi, who
lived in a pā on the coast. Korongoi led a raid on the giant's pā, but was
badly defeated and was captured. Toaangina cut his body into pieces and

displayed the body parts to passers-by as a warning of what would happen to any who opposed him. Then he put the chief's remains into a kono oi (waterproof basket) and floated it across the river. It was a painful sight for Huiawarua, the daughter of the dead chief, who lived at Te Auaunga pā (near Akaaka), across the river from the giant's pā.

She vehemently urged her husband, a young rangatira named Te Horeta, to avenge her father's death. But Te Horeta knew only too well how powerful their enemy was. Although valiant in battle he preferred to fight with men with whom he was more evenly matched. After he had made a raid on a neighbouring village he returned flushed with victory and boasted to his wife of his prowess. She was a woman of singular purpose. Instead of flattering him she reproached him once again for refusing to avenge her father, accusing the warrior of faint-heartedness and lack of love for her.

Te Horeta had no reply to make to these charges. Sick at heart he returned to his whare and lay down with his face to the wall, refusing food and making no reply to those who spoke to him. Huiawarua took no notice of him. She refused to speak to him until he avenged her father's death, even when her people begged her to rouse him from his torpor. Ten days went by, during which Te Horeta tasted no food and spoke no word to those who addressed him.

News of his condition was conveyed to his uncle, Pāpaka, in his home on the shores of the Manukau Harbour. He hastened to his nephew's pā, where he found Te Horeta lying silent on his mat. Pāpaka could see that his nephew was in a bad way.

'We have sought an answer from the atua of the air and the land and the sea,' he said, 'but we have received no reply. From this it appears that the thing that troubles you comes not from these causes, but from something inside you. If there is something you have done that shames you, tell me, and we will see that wrongs are righted.'

Finally Te Horeta broke his silence, asking his wife to fill a calabash of water for their guest.

'Do not take it from the river, but go to the spring for the water there is cooler and clearer.'

Huiawarua picked up the calabash and made the journey to the distant spring of water. When she had gone Te Horeta spoke to his uncle.

'I have lost my mana,' he said simply. 'I am ready to face any warrior, but my wife has asked me to avenge the death of Korongoi by killing Toaangina. This I cannot do, for I fear him and I am ashamed.'

'I will help you,' Pāpaka said. 'Your mana will be restored, for Toaangina cannot be destroyed by a single warrior. It needs the co-operation of many powerful chiefs and you will be among them. Let Huiawarua bring food and water to me and my men, and then we will depart. When we return your mana will be restored.'

When she heard of the plans that were being made, Huiawarua was content. She brought food and drink for Pāpaka and his men and for her husband, who by this time had recovered his spirits.

Pāpaka went to a pā near Manurewa to visit the ariki Rangikaimataī. When Pāpaka was seen approaching the pā, the umu were prepared for a feast. Rangikaimataī welcomed him to his whare, took off his dogskin cloak and laid it on the ground as a mat for his visitor. Pāpaka lay down on his back on the edge of the cloak as an indication of his inferiority to the great chief. He gazed up at the roof and recited a karakia, which was also a challenge:

> There are four strands
> Holding the roof of the house,
> With more to come.
> Is there a man braver or stronger
> Than Toaangina?
> He holds the power to overcome the wind,
> To overcome the water,
> To overcome the forest,
> To overcome the sun,
> To overcome the stars,
> To overcome the sea,
> To overcome men.

Rangikaimataī looked down at him with a twinkle in his eye. 'No, my son, he is only a hawk that wheels endlessly in the sky and has no nest to sit on.

I, the chief hawk of Tāmaki, have a nest to sit on.'

Pāpaka gave a satisfied smile, rose up from the cloak and took a courteous leave of Rangikaimataī, without waiting for the ovens to be opened. He travelled straight onwards until he came to the great pā at Maungakiekie (One Tree Hill), where he was received in a similar manner by the ariki Rangihauhautū. From the edge of the chief's cloak he again repeated the karakia and said, 'Tē rite tangata ki a Toaangina, Toaangina te wai, Toaangina te ahi, Toaangina te tangata,' which may be translated, 'No one is equal to Toaangina, Toaangina is master of water, Toaangina is master of fire, Toaangina is master of men.'

Then Pāpaka heard the proud reply of an ariki: 'No, my son, Toaangina is only a dog with a spotted skin. He is a mongrel, but we are the white dogs of Tāmaki. They can see us in the dark.'

Pāpaka hurried back to his own pā. 'I have spoken to the ariki of Manurewa and Maungakiekie,' he told them. 'If we go to fight the giant Toaangina of Waikato and are defeated, we will be avenged by Rangikaimataī and Rangihauhautū. They will not let him escape. But to us first the glory and the hazard. Who will come with me?'

A great shout rose from the toa, and every able-bodied man stepped forward eagerly.

'It is well,' said Pāpaka. 'I will choose a taua of 70 from among you.'

Loaded with the war party, the waka taua sped down a long arm of the Manukau Harbour. Then it had to be dragged overland, launched on the Waikato River and paddled to Te Horeta's pā. The command of the canoe was given to Te Horeta himself. He ordered the men to lie down in the bilge, and the women covered them with flax. The only one who remained in sight, holding the steering paddle, was Te Awa, the father-in-law of Toaangina, who had long since become disgusted with the giant's cruelty. He dug the paddle deep in the water, the prow swung out from the shore and the canoe floated majestically down the river.

Toaangina was swinging idly on the vine scanning the river when he saw the huge canoe with its single occupant floating downstream. His suspicions were roused. As soon as the canoe drew level with him, he swung far out over the water until he was able to look down directly into the hull.

With shock he recognised the steersman, but could think of no reason why such a valuable war canoe should be in the hands of one man. The returning vine carried him to the riverbank, but a mighty thrust brought it level with the canoe again.

'Why do you come alone in this canoe and why are you bringing these bundles of flax?' he demanded.

Te Awa made no reply. He turned the canoe so that it headed towards the bank. There was something sinister about the empty, silent war canoe and Toaangina's nerve broke. He dropped quickly from the vine and ran to his whare, looking over his shoulder. He saw that the bow of the canoe had touched the bank. Suddenly a tremendous shout came from the canoe, the flax bundles were tossed aside and the warriors sprang out and raced towards him.

Toaangina darted frantically through the pā with the bloodthirsty toa not far behind. Some of them engaged Toaangina's warriors in combat, but Te Horeta with a chosen few took no notice of them and continued the chase. Toaangina swerved and raced back towards the canoe.

'Have mercy on me,' he gasped. 'What shall I do?'

Te Awa, who was still sitting in the canoe, spoke no word, but pointed to a path that ran through a raupō swamp. The giant raced onwards, with Te Horeta and his men rapidly gaining on him. Toaangina was forced to expend his strength in flattening the rushes, thus making an easy path for his pursuers. As they came closer he veered to one side and managed to reach a mound of dry ground. He turned to face his foes and relief swept over him. His challenger was only the coward and weakling Te Horeta, the son-in-law of the man he had killed.

But it was a different Te Horeta who faced him that day. Inflamed with rage, the young man thrust fiercely with his taiaha and drew blood. The maddened giant swung his own taiaha, as long and thick as a tree, at his opponent, but it whistled harmlessly above his head. He tried to lower it, but each time the young chief ducked beneath the blow.

Te Horeta was unable to repeat his first success. His weapon caught in the thickly clustered raupō, while Toaangina's great height allowed him to swing his taiaha freely and to beat downwards against the young man.

Taking advantage of a momentary pause, Te Horeta thrust the end of

his weapon in the ground, held the tongue firmly in his hands and broke the staff with a strong kick. The deadly pointed tongue was like a short spear or sword. He ran in under Toaangina's guard and jabbed the point into his heart. Like a great tōtara, the giant fell back, lifeless.

Te Horeta bent over the body and was busy for a few moments before rushing away in search of Toaangina's son, whom he quickly despatched.

When the battle was over and the giant's followers had been defeated, the warriors gathered around the body of Toaangina. Te Wehe, one of the toa, stood by it, claiming triumphantly that he had overcome the scourge of the river.

'But it was I who killed him,' Te Horeta said.

Te Wehe laughed scornfully. 'It is easy to make such a claim, but you have just arrived. I killed him and I have proof of it.'

'Show us the proof, then,' said one of the older men.

Te Wehe's broad smile proclaimed his confidence.

'Here it is,' he said, holding up a greenstone tiki that was recognised by everyone as Toaangina's property.

The heads of the warriors all turned to Te Horeta, expecting to find him overcome with confusion; but the young chief addressed Te Wehe.

'Open Toaangina's mouth,' he commanded. 'What do you see?'

'He has no tongue,' Te Wehe said in surprise.

'Do you know what has become of it?'

'No.'

Te Horeta drew his hand from inside his cloak and held out the severed tongue of Toaangina.

Te Wehe recognised that his deceit had been revealed, but he was not disconcerted.

'You have proved that you have killed him. You can have him, but I will have his land.'

The chief dismissed the matter contemptuously. 'We are one family. We will not quarrel over a small thing.'

In the circumstances the matter of land was of no concern to Te Horeta. What was infinitely more important was that his mana was restored and his wife had regained her earlier admiration of his manhood. It may be proof of their reconciliation that there were seven children from their marriage.

Rongokako

Rongokako was the son of Tamatea-mai-tawhiti and was therefore of noble birth. He was sent by his people from the East Coast to a noted wharekura in the Wairarapa, but he did not distinguish himself there. In fact he had to be removed on a number of occasions because he had fallen asleep while instruction was being given by the tohunga, Tāwhai, who considered Rongokako a failure.

When it came to the time of the tests at the end of the period of instruction, Rongokako was not given the opportunity to take part. The final proof of the candidate's ability was to take giant strides to travel rapidly from one place to another. Rongokako sought permission to take part but was refused as he had not undergone any of the other tests.

Tāwhai listened attentively as the candidates recited the preliminary karakia. If a candidate was able to recite them without faltering or making mistakes, he was told to bring back a piece of rimurapa (seaweed) from an offshore island as proof of his ability to travel in giant strides. Only a few candidates successfully completed the karakia and were sent to fetch the rimurapa. Each one returned with a piece of rimupuka, which caused a great deal of head-shaking on the part of the tohunga. The rimurapa was live kelp, which grew only on the rocky coast of the offshore islands, while rimupuka was composed of strands that had broken away and had been washed on to the mainland and dried in the sun. The tohunga could therefore tell at a glance that the young men had been unable to cross from the shore to the islands.

When Rongokako saw that no one had been successful, he again begged permission to undergo the test. Possibly because of his noble ancestry, the head tohunga gave his permission and, to the surprise of his teachers, he repeated the karakia correctly and without hesitation. He set out on his journey and when he returned to the wharekura the rimurapa that he carried in his hand was still wet with sea water. After this feat his acceptance as a tohunga was assured and he was anointed with oil.

Rongokako's feat had not endeared him to the other students, who determined that they would conquer him in the arts of love. Many of the young men had set their affections on Muriwhenua, a puhi of Hauraki, whose beauty and charm were known throughout most of the North Island. A number of the young men manned canoes and set off northwards, skirting the east coast, to woo the young woman. Chief among them was Pāoa, who was the most skilled in navigation and the handling of canoes.

Pāoa chivalrously offered a seat in the canoe to Rongokako though he knew him to be a rival, but the newly fledged tohunga declined. He waited until Pāoa was out of sight and some distance up the coast. Then he made a gigantic stride that took him many kilometres on his northward journey. He walked along the beach until the canoe came level with him. Pāoa concealed his surprise and again offered to take him on board. Once more Rongokako refused and took another step, which carried him to Te Matau-a-Māui (Cape Kidnappers). His footstep can still be seen there in the rock. From there he went on to Māhia Peninsula and then to Whāngārā.

When Pāoa saw his rival for the third time he realised that he was being played with. He encouraged his paddlers to put on a spurt and landed some distance north of Tokomaru Bay, where he prepared a tāwhiti (trap). Rongokako saw it in time and set it off with his foot. The taratara (setting stick) flew high in the air and plummeted down to earth in Waikato, where it took root and grew into a tree. Rongokako passed swiftly onwards, reaching Hauraki well in advance of his rival. There he was successful in his wooing and he married Muriwhenua.

Other stories attribute superhuman feats to Rongokako. In one of them he was a giant who had injured many people. As he paid a visit to the East Cape, accompanied by a huge kiwi (or moa), Pāoa attempted to destroy him and to capture his bird. Pāoa must also have been of gigantic stature, for he cut a tree and planted the trunk at Mount Hikurangi and then bent it over until its top was pegged to the hill between Tokomaru and Waipiro bays. A rope noose was tied to the treetop and the place where it was fixed was known thereafter as Tāwhiti-a-Pāoa (The snare of Pāoa).

As Rongokako travelled northwards, his tapuwae (footsteps) were printed indelibly at Māhia Peninsula and Whāngārā, while the mark of the kiwi's foot was left at the junction of the Waikanae Stream and the Tūranganui River. When the giant saw the snare he raised his staff and tripped it. As it sprang back the mountain was shattered and formed the three hills known as Aorangimaunga, Honokau and Taetae. The rope that formed the noose snaked out in a westerly direction and, as it sank to earth and lay on the ground, it became the Arowhana mountain ridge. Striding seawards, Rongokako left his last footprint on the rocks at Horoera, near East Cape, before returning to Hawaiki.

Tamarau

The story of Tamarau begins far back in time, when Ngāhue came to Aotearoa in search of Pounamu (Greenstone). Ngāhue was followed by Hape, who visited Tūhua (Mayor Island), where he knew that Pounamu had taken refuge, but found that it had been driven away by the tūhua (obsidian) of that island. Pounamu had fled to the South Island, but at the time Hape was not aware of this. He followed one report after another. The first took him to Whakaari (White Island), but Pounamu had been frightened by the boiling springs and the trembling of the ground and had continued its flight. After leaving Whakaari, Hape settled for a while at Ōhiwa with his family. When he resumed the search he took the mauri of the kūmara with him, thus rendering the crops infertile.

Hape's quest took him to many parts of the North Island. At Mount Tarawera he blocked the steam with a huge rock, known as Te Tatau-a-Hape (the door of Hape). He crossed the Kāingaroa Plains, came to the source of the Rangitāiki River and then to the Rangitīkei, which he descended, eventually reaching Porirua Harbour. Passing over Raukawa (Cook Strait) and landing at Wairau, he travelled to Kaikōura, crossed Kā Tiritiri o te Moana (the Southern Alps) and reached Te Tai Poutini (the West Coast), where he built a whare. He learned that Ngāhue had returned to Hawaiki with some pieces of pounamu, but that great quantities remained. Hape stayed in that place until he died. His body was left in the whare, which became overgrown with māwhai and pōhue (convolvulus).

Meanwhile, his sons became concerned because the kūmara crops came to nothing. When this happened several seasons in succession they realised that their father had taken the mauri with him. They decided to find him and recover it. There were two sons, Rāwaho, the elder, whose birth was miraculous for he had issued from his mother's armpit, and Tamarau. They followed their father's footsteps, past Tarawera and on to Porirua Harbour. There they met some local people and made enquiries.

'We are searching for a man who came this way. His hair was tied in eight knots and he had two belts. Have you seen him?'

'What are the names of the belts?' they were asked.

'One was Rāwaho and the other Tamarau.'

'Yes, he has been here, but he has crossed over Raukawa.'

The brothers called on the atua Te Pōtūmai and Te Pōtahurikē to carry them over the strait. From information they received they came at last to the place of the pounamu. They were told that Hape had lived and died there and that his remains still lay in the whare he had built.

Rāwaho, who was a tohunga of considerable power, began to prepare for the ordeal of finding Hape's body by chanting incantations, but the younger brother pushed on recklessly. Using a charm to aid him, he pulled aside the creeping māwhai and pōhue and entered the whare, where he found his father's shrivelled body. He bent down and took Hape's ear between his teeth. By this act his father's mana entered into him and he became an atua.

In this way Tamarau gained greater mana than his brother Rāwaho. He took the belts that were named after his brother and himself and contained the mauri of the kūmara, and tied them around his body, where they were hidden by his cloak. He also took some of his father's hair as the tangible evidence of Hape's wairua and placed it in the belt Rāwaho.

He went out into the sunshine and found his brother still engaged in the ritual that would allow him to approach his father's body.

'That time is past,' Tamarau told him. 'End your incantations now and go in to our father.'

Rāwaho did so and saw that his brother had bitten his father's ear. He knew from this that Hape's wairua had already passed to Tamarau and that his younger brother also possessed the mauri of the kūmara. There was nothing left for him to do but to salute his father by stooping down and pressing his nose against his father's.

After this the brothers returned to the North Island. At Arorangi, a hill

near Waiohau (on the Rangitāiki River, south of Te Teko), they sat down and ate food to rid themselves of their tapu. A quarrel broke out between them over who was to carry the food. Tamarau yielded to his elder brother, who went on alone. No sooner had he left than Tamarau, endowed with his father's power, rose into the air and flew over his brother's head. To his amazement, Rāwaho saw Tamarau's reflection in the water of a swamp as he plodded on.

Tamarau touched down several times but flew on as soon as his brother caught up with him. On one occasion he dropped a tī kōuka tree that he had carried with him from the South Island. The tree took root and eventually became known as Tī-whaka-aweawe, the wandering cabbage tree of the Kāingaroa Plains.

Rāwaho ended his journey at Ōhiwa and began to cultivate the kūmara there. To his delight its fertility had returned. This was due to Tamarau's magnanimity, for it was he who owned the mauri and conferred its benefits on his brother's crops.

Thereafter Tamarau continued to travel by air. Often his brother would plod laboriously after him, preparing new kūmara plantations. The younger brother was in later years regarded as a war god, whose appearance was usually that of a pākura (swamp hen), and occasionally that of a meteor.

HEROES AND DEEDS OF DARING

The following stories give us an insight into the traditional Māori world view, including the relationship of people to the environment. For Māori, the material world and the spirit world co-existed. Although there are aspects of everyday life in the following stories, there is a supernatural element in them all.

The Mana of Kahurangi

Kahurangi means 'treasured possession' and was applied to high-born women, as well as to a variety of pounamu (greenstone) that is a translucent green with pale flecks running through it.

It was also the name of an ancestress of the Waikato people who lived on the shores of the Hauraki Gulf. From the spirit world she watched closely over the affairs of her descendants and was grieved when they neglected to perform the rites and ceremonies that were pleasing to the atua. So great was her concern over their carelessness and indifference that she gained permission from the guardians of Rarohenga to return to her own people.

She entered their pā and accompanied a party who were performing a ceremony by a stream. At the conclusion a light enveloped them and Kahurangi was changed into a huge rock. The people realised that the rock must be a manifestation of their ancestress, who stood at the border of their territory as a warning and as a protection against invasion.

Shortly afterwards an old woman of the tribe went to the stream and, impelled by curiosity, made her way through the water up to the rock. It was a violation of Kahurangi's tapu. The sky was covered with clouds, lightning flickered around the sacred rock and thunder rolled closely overhead. When the storm abated the rock was no longer there. Kahurangi had departed for her home in the spirit world.

The old woman who had driven the ancestress away was afflicted with an unbearable pain in her armpit. She rushed into a swamp, splashing water over herself in her attempts to gain relief. When the pain subsided she found that the mana of Kahurangi had entered into her. One of the symptoms of her new-found power was the ability to climb trees, which caused a great deal of laughter among her people.

At this time the members of the leading hapū of Waikato experienced some ill-fortune. They were suffering from disease, a poor growing season and enemy raids. They sought the assistance of their principal tohunga. After consulting with the atua, he told them that they would shortly be visited by their people from the coastal pā and that among them would be an old woman named Tokawhakatete. It was she who was the cause of their present misfortunes because she had violated the tapu of their protectress Kahurangi.

'The mana of our ancestress is embedded in her armpit,' he told them. 'Until it is returned to Kahurangi we shall never prosper. This is what you must do.

'Do not lose sight of Tokawhakatete. If you follow my instructions you will be able to return the mana that belongs to Kahurangi and our tribe will be saved.

'Toka will go down to the stream to bathe and to subdue the irritation of her armpit. When she has done this she will sit on the sand in the middle of a ring of red berries. As soon as she sits down you must rush out from your hiding places and gather up the berries before she is able to touch them. She will then be powerless.

'Take her back to the whare. Light a fire of rātā leaves and tell her to reveal her knowledge to you. If she refuses, drop the berries into the fire one by one. As the last berry is consumed in the flames, hold up her left arm and you will see the sign of the mana of Kahurangi. Place a piece of rātā bark on it and the symbol will be transferred to the wood.

'This, my children, is only the beginning of your task, but unless you do this, the gods will never favour us again.'

They did everything that the tohunga had told them. The mana was transferred to a piece of rātā bark, and Tokawhakatete, relieved of her intolerable burden but feeling empty and exhausted, leaped from a high cliff to her death.

While this was happening, the tohunga was explaining a dream to the elders.

'The atua have revealed to me that my daughter must marry the chief who is visiting us now,' he told them. 'Do not oppose this marriage, my people. In due course a girl will be born of their union, and through her the mana of Kahurangi will return to Waikato.'

The marriage was celebrated, but afterwards the young chief was alarmed to find that his wife refused to eat, sitting silently on her mat in the whare.

'What is troubling you?' he asked.

She was reluctant to tell him, but he persuaded her.

'It is because of the dream that my father had. Our people have buried a piece of bark that is tapu. It must be dug up — and then I have a long and dangerous task to perform.'

'I will share it with you if it will lighten your burden,' her husband said. 'Let us begin the task now.'

Accompanied by many of the tribespeople who were carrying offerings to the tapu rātā bark, they went to the place where it was buried. The young woman's hair was cut off and spread on the ground; the bark was then dug up and placed on her head. She gave a long wail as the remaining hair was burnt off her scalp at the touch of the bark, but the people sighed with relief, for it was evident that the bark was still alive and imbued with the mana of Kahurangi.

The young couple set out on their quest, carrying the bark with them. They travelled for many days, guided by the bark, and at length came to a place where no water could be found. The young woman lay down, exhausted and parched with thirst. They had been searching for water for a long time and had come to the end of their endurance.

Her husband, who was sitting beside her, picked up a stone and idly threw it into the bush. To his astonishment he heard a splash as though the stone had fallen into water. He picked up his wife in his arms and hurried in the direction of the sound. Bursting through the bushes he found himself on the brink of a deep, still lake. He gave his wife a drink and bathed her head. The girl revived quickly. She gathered tītoki leaves and threw them into the pool in gratitude for her recovery.

As the young people sat side by side, they saw a bright light shining on the far side of the lake. They attempted to lift the wooden casket in which the bark was hidden, but it had become so heavy that they were unable to move it, by which sign they knew that their quest was nearly at an end. Night had fallen, but the light guided them as they made their way around the lake. Suddenly the light disappeared and they were left in impenetrable darkness.

They heard the wailing of a child and clung together, fearful of what might happen next. Then the light shone out again, close to them. In it they saw a vision of a baby — and knew that they had found the birthplace of Kahurangi. Together they chanted prayers of thankfulness and petition. The face of the old tohunga, who had died before they set out on their journey, also appeared in the light. He was smiling in spite of the tears that ran down his tattooed cheeks. 'As you see my tears,' he said, 'so it shall be with your child.'

When daylight came they collected the casket and returned to their people with it as quickly as they could.

The final challenge had not yet come to them, nor was their quest completed.

Soon afterwards a baby girl was born to them. She seemed bathed in light and an atmosphere of awe and foreboding filled the pā. Day after day storms raged and the atua of earth and sky seemed to be at war, yet through the crash of the thunder and the blinding flashes of lightning the child lay serene and quiet, whether asleep or awake.

On the sixth day the infant spoke. She said, 'Do not be sorrowful for me. My tears will be your protection. They will show my love for my people.'

Early on the morning of the seventh day the wairua of the baby left its body and went to its final resting place. When the mother went to look at her, even the body was gone. In its place lay a piece of pounamu, clear as the water of the forest pool, shaped like a tear. It was called Kahurangi. It was a gift from the divine ancestress Kahurangi, the visible sign of her mana that would preserve the prosperity of the people of Waikato so long as it was guarded and cherished by them.

Taukata
and Hoaki

Sometime after Toi had come to Aotearoa, two brothers, Taukata and
Hoaki, left Hawaiki in the Tūtarakauika canoe, which some say was made
of pumice. They were looking for their sister Kanioro, who had travelled
to Aotearoa with her husband Pourangahua.

Taukata and Hoaki landed at Whakatāne. As they stood on the beach
feeling the sand under their feet and the sun warm on their bodies after
their long journey, they chanted a karakia. The chant was heard by a young
woman named Te Kurawhakaata who lived in the hill fort Kaputerangi,
built long before by Toi. She told her father Tama-ki-hikurangi, the chief
of the pā, that there were two strangers on the beach. When Te Kura told
him the news, he ordered her to go down to the beach and invite the two
young men to visit them.

Te Kura went down to the beach and greeted the strangers.

'My father invites you to Kaputerangi,' she said. 'Where have you
come from?'

'From Mataora in far Hawaiki,' they said.

When it was known that Hoaki and Taukata had come from the
homeland, a feast was prepared to do honour to them. Women began to
pound fern root in preparation for the meal. Hoaki heard the sound of the
pounders and demanded suspiciously, 'What is that sound I hear?'

Tama-ki-hikurangi looked at him curiously, for it seemed a strange
question. 'It is only the women beating the aruhe,' he said.

Later, when the meal was served, the guests looked with interest at the vegetables that were placed in wooden bowls with the flesh foods. Besides the aruhe there were hīnau and tawa berries and the tender tips of the leaves of the mamaku and tī kōuka. When they tasted them they were disappointed.

'Is the kūmara of our homeland not to be found in Aotearoa?' they asked their hosts.

'No,' said Tama. 'These are the products of the forest. They are our daily food.'

One brother remarked to the other as they continued their meal, 'We are eating wood today.'

Tama overheard the remark and was indignant. 'These are the foods left to us by our ancestor Toi.'

Taukata replied shortly, 'Then your ancestor must have eaten wood,' and so Toitehuatahi became known as Toikairākau (Toi the wood eater).

When the meal was over the brothers looked at each other and knew what they must do. Taukata asked for some water. When it was brought to him he took some kao (dried cooked kūmara) from his belt, powdered it and mixed it to a paste. He handed it to Tama-ki-hikurangi and to the other people, saying, 'The best foods indeed are at Hawaiki.'

It was a memorable occasion. Having once tasted kūmara the people of Kaputerangi could not be content until they had procured seed and could establish their own plantations. The possibility of a long canoe voyage was discussed, but they had no seaworthy canoe.

The two brothers scouted along the beach and soon Taukata returned with the news that near Ōpihi he had discovered a log that could be adzed into an ocean-going canoe. He and Hoaki worked on it with three prized adzes: Te Manokuha, Te Waiheke and Te Warawara-tai-o-Tāne. When it was finished the canoe was given the descriptive name Te Aratāwhao (the driftwood path).

Taukata remained behind with his new friends, Te Hapūoneone of the Kaputerangi pā, but Hoaki was accompanied by Tama-ki-hikurangi and many other warriors. It was an eventful voyage. Tama was greatly feared by some of his people. He was a noted tohunga; with such a person on board, who could tell what might happen to the voyagers? Before they left they planned to kill him, but Tama overheard their plot. He hid the bailer, bored a hole in the bottom of the canoe and plugged it up again.

When the canoe was out of sight of land Tama pulled the stopper out of the hole and the water rushed in and began to fill the canoe. A frantic search was made for the bailer and it was only when it seemed that they would all be drowned that Tama produced it. He recited many karakia, some to assist the bailing, some to bind the canoe firmly together and others to calm the winds and waves. After this demonstration of power, Tama-ki-hikurangi had no need to repeat the lesson and he was unmolested.

When the canoe arrived at Hawaiki, Hoaki received a welcome from his own people, and the men of Te Hapūoneone were included. Many tales of Aotearoa were told in the meeting house at night and on sunny days by the lagoon at Pikopiko-i-whiti, until imaginations were fired and it was decided that a fleet of canoes should be built to take a colony of people to the far-off land.

The kūmara tubers were carried on the Mātaatua canoe, on which all the men of Te Hapūoneone returned. Hoaki remained behind in the homeland and gave the following message to his friends when they departed: 'When you reach your home you must build a whata to hold your kūmara crop. Wait till the summer is over and the harvest is gathered. Then you must take my brother Taukata to the whata and kill him, so that his blood is spilled in the storehouse. If you do this, the prized product of Hawaiki will never depart from you.'

As Hoaki had said, so it was done and the kūmara remained forever in the new land. The mauri (life-force) of the kūmara was retained. Taukata's skull was preserved for many generations. It was placed at the edge of the plantation with a seed kūmara in each eye socket and maintained a jealous watch over the cultivations.

A proverb that applies to appetising food secured at great cost is: 'Te iti oneone i kapunga mai i Hawaiki.' ('A little bit of soil brought in the hollow of the hand from Hawaiki.')

The Finding of
Tau-tini-awhitia

Huru-mā-angiangi was expecting a child and craved the flesh of birds. She said to her husband, Porouanoano, 'Porou, I would like a plump bird for my evening meal.'

Porou went into the forest to see what he could find. Strangely, there were no weka or tūī or kererū, but he managed to catch a huia and a kōtuku and brought them home alive. His wife was greatly taken with the unusual birds and refused to have them killed.

'I would like to keep them as pets,' she said.

Shortly after this Porou deserted his wife and went to live at another pā where he married for a second time. In due course Huru gave birth to a boy whom she named Tau-tini-awhitia. His mother lavished all her affection on him and he grew into a strong, healthy lad. He excelled at games such as canoe racing, whipping tops and running races, and also at catching and spearing birds.

The other boys became jealous of him. One day they taunted him because he had no father, saying, 'The deeds of the fatherless boy are most successful.' Tautini was upset. He ran home to his mother, crying, and asked her: 'Mother, where is my father?'

'Your father is not here, Tautini,' she was forced to say. 'He has gone a long way from home. Tomorrow morning, if you look toward the rising sun, you will see the direction he went.'

The boy went away thoughtful. He said nothing to his mother, but walked into the forest and picked up the seedpod of a rewarewa. He took it to a stream and put it in the water. He was delighted to find that it remained upright.

He went back to his mother's whare and confronted her. 'Mother, I have made up my mind to leave home. I am going to look for my father.'

Huru begged him to stay with her but Tautini had resolved to leave. 'I cannot stay here after what the other boys have said. I am ashamed.'

She saw that he could not be dissuaded. 'Son,' she said, although her heart was breaking, 'remain just a little while. You must do what you must, but wait until I cook some food for you to take on your journey. You have a long way to go and you must keep up your strength.'

'No,' he said. 'I cannot wait. A spear thrust can be parried, but the thrust of cruel words cannot be avoided. I must escape while I can.'

She gave him her blessing and Tautini embarked on the seedpod canoe and sailed out to sea, protected by a charm that his mother chanted:

> From whom is this canoe?
> From whom is this canoe?
> From me — mine.
> From Uru-mā-angiangi,
> From Tara-mā-angiangi.
> The cunning snares of Rei
> Are as nothing to all
> The canoes gliding swiftly.
>
> Let the threatening winds coming hither
> Be all stayed.
> Pass through space,
> Pass through gloom,
> Pass through billows.
> Lo! the earth glides by.
> Sail on to the good landing.
> Now land quietly, gently, thus.
> A canoe lightly passing over waves
> The passing away, such as now,
> I behold with satisfaction.

Guided by his mother's incantation, Tautini's canoe came to the village where the boy's father lived. He drew his canoe up on to the beach and covered it with gravel so that no one could find it.

The children of the kāinga had seen Tautini arrive in the strange canoe and they raced down to the beach to claim him as a slave. They surrounded him and marched him up to the village. A clamour arose as the older people joined with the children in squabbling over him, each wanting to claim him.

By this time Porouanoano had had a son by his second wife. He was only a small boy but he was full of self-importance. Because of his father's mana he was successful in obtaining Tautini as his slave, little knowing that the bigger boy was his half-brother. The little lad ran up to his father shouting gleefully, 'Old man! See, I have a new slave.'

Porou was pleased with his son's triumph and said, 'Very good. But take him away and let him live among the bushes. He must not come inside the whare.'

A few days later, while the children were at play, Tautini went into the forest and caught a huia and a kōtuku alive. He kept them hidden among the bushes and taught them to repeat two short sentences. The huia learned to say, 'The fire is not burning brightly — dark, dark, darkness prevails.' The kōtuku's sentence was, 'The fire does not blaze — it is very dark in here.'

Late one night Tautini crept quietly into the wharepuni. He looked around and saw that everyone was asleep. He went and fetched the two birds in the wicker cages he had made for them and set them down by the dying embers of the fire.

The huia cried loudly, 'The fire is not burning brightly — dark, dark, darkness prevails.'

Its voice woke the sleeping men and women and, at that moment, the kōtuku cried in its harsh voice, 'The fire does not blaze — it is very dark in here.'

Porou bounded to his feet and examined the birds curiously. His eyes fell on Tautini, who stood silently in front of him. He said slowly: 'There is no doubt that this is not a slave, but my son. These are the kind of birds his mother longed for before he was born.'

He pressed his son's nose in greeting and wept tears of joy. When morning came he took Tautini down to the river. There he chanted incantations and performed the ceremonies that were suited to the son of a chief, and received him with honour into the midst of the people.

Tamarereti

Tamarereti had observed the kurakura (*Aurora Australis* or Southern Lights) and announced that he would sail south to find out what caused them. Under his direction a tōtara log was hollowed out, and provided with top-strakes and magnificently carved prow- and stern-pieces that were inlaid with iridescent pāua shell, and bedecked with long trailing plumes. When completed the canoe was named Te Rua-o-Māhu.

Seventy young chiefs volunteered for the expedition. To their number were added two aged tohunga who were experienced in navigation and in the karakia that would preserve the explorers from danger. The canoe was fully provisioned and set out on its southward journey.

The people of Tamarereti's tribe waited as the months passed, but nothing was seen or heard of Te Rua-o-Māhu or its crew. Finally, one stormy night they saw a canoe, obviously in distress, being driven towards the rock-bound coast. The alarm was sounded and soon the shore was lined with people. They watched while the helpless canoe was lifted high on the crest of a wave and hurled against the teeth of the rocks. Presently the bodies of dead men were washed ashore and everyone knew that Tamarereti had brought his canoe home. His body and that of many toa was laid gently on the wet sand. They had been cruelly torn and mangled by the pounding waves. The only ones who still nourished the flickering spark of life in their bodies were the two old tohunga. They were carried to the fire, warmed and given food and drink. Slowly the life came back into them and they were able to give an account of their adventures.

The canoe had travelled southwards for many weeks until it came to a precipitous wall of ice cliffs. The white sea pounded the base of the wall and masses of ice groaned and creaked at the foot of the cliffs. As they cruised up and down the days grew shorter, until the sun disappeared and darkness continued, lit only by the faint light of the stars.

One of the old men chanted feebly:

> The world of the south
> Spread abroad there
> With its mountainous ranges
> The cliffs of ice
> And the pattern fish
> And wonders before which I prostrate myself.

Then the darkness was dispelled by Ngā Kurakura-o-Hine-nui-te-pō (the glowing lights of the great goddess of the night). Cold flames leaped from earth to sky and descended to the earth again. The very air crackled and appeared as though it was on fire. It steamed and smoked and gave out a smell like that of burning flax.

From time to time they caught fish to augment their food supplies. While eating a shrimp that had been taken from the stomach of a fish, Tamarereti choked. 'He paku te ika i raoa ai a Tamarereti' ('It was a small fish that choked Tamarereti'), the old man said — a saying that has become a proverb. The leader's body was embalmed and brought back. They were weak with privation, hunger and cold by the time they neared home. When they were within sight of land they had no strength to fight the storm that had risen. The young men were drowned as the canoe was driven on to the rocks. Only the old men who had been cared for and sheltered from the worst of the weather on the homeward voyage had managed to survive and come safely to land.

The storm died down and the canoe was recovered. Driftwood was piled high on the beach and Te Rua-o-Māhu was placed on top of the heap. In it were the bodies of the drowned men. Tamarereti's body was placed in the centre of the canoe. It was clad in fine cloaks and in his cold hand he held a pouwhenua (a taiaha-like weapon). The driftwood was kindled at night and before long the canoe was wreathed in flames. To the solemn chants of the tribal tohunga, the wairua of Tamarereti and his men left their bodies in the glory of the leaping flames. The canoe and all its contents were reduced to smouldering embers and ashes, but the spirit or essence was transferred to the sky.

The bowpiece became the stars of the Southern Cross, which were named Te Pūtea-iti-a-Tamarereti (The little finely-woven basket of Tamarereti). The canoe itself spread out across the sky, reaching as far as Autahi (Canopus), the pāua shell that decorated the sternpost. Te Taura-o-te-punga (The anchor rope) became the Pointers and Te Punga-o-te-waka-o-Tamarereti (The anchor of the canoe) became the Dark Hole. It was only when the tohunga told the story of the perils of the voyage and the sights that had been seen that the *Aurora Australis* became known as Ngā Kurakura-o-Hine-nui-te-pō.

Tautoru the Hunter

Tautoru was a young man noted not only for his ability as a bird-hunter, but also for his ingenuity in devising a snare that was so effective that in one day he could catch so many kererū that 20 men were needed to carry them. He set scented flowers and succulent berries around the snare and attracted birds to it from far and near. Kererū, kākā and tūī were caught in his famous trap. The tapu kawau that was turned to stone and stands in the tide rips of Te Aumiti (French Pass) was named Kawau-a-Toru for him. He also trained kurī to hunt ground birds such as kiwi and weka.

With all this natural ability and resourcefulness, Tautoru remained modest and unassuming, giving thanks to Tāne and reciting the appropriate karakia. It was this quality that endeared him especially to Rauroha, a female spirit of the overworlds. She visited him each night and spent the hours of darkness with him; but when, accidentally or by design, he looked on her face, she was forced to leave him, for it was forbidden for mortals to gaze on her beauty.

Tautoru set about his work with a sorrowful heart. He grieved for the divine woman who had been his bride. In setting his snare near the top of a tree he became careless and fell to the ground, breaking his neck.

From her home in the heavens Rauroha saw a huge company of birds gathered at one spot in the forest and knew that it must be the place where her mortal love had set his snare. Of Tautoru himself she could see no sign until she looked down and saw him lying motionless on the ground. She descended and wept over his body.

When Tautoru's friends discovered him they lifted him on to a litter and carried him through the forest. He was placed in a sitting position, dressed in rich garments. But when the bearers neared their village, the body was no longer on the litter. In some mysterious fashion it had been removed unseen by his friends. The tohunga declared that Tāne, who had loved this young man, had taken his body to his home in the overworlds. And so it may have been; but we can be sure that the wairua of Tautoru was welcomed by Rauroha.

In the constellation of Orion, Tautoru can be seen in the act of snaring the kererū. The principal star cluster Puarangarua is the mass of berries and flowers with which he decorated his snare. Rigel is Te Pua-tāwhiwhi-o-Tautoru (The berry bloom of Tautoru). The star beneath it is Te Tuke-o-Tautoru (The elbow of Tautoru), while Te Pewa-o-Tautoru is the arm and a row of stars forms Te Tata-o-Tautoru (The apron of Tautoru). The row of three central stars (The belt of Orion) is Tautoru (Settled three). On clear nights multitudes of tiny kererū (The nebula in Orion) can be seen winging their way to the pua (blossoms) of the snare of Tautoru.

The Abduction of Rona

Rona had 45 suitors in her own tribe and others of whom she was unaware. Among these were Hākawau of Kāwhia, who admired her from a distance but had never declared his love, and Pāwa, an evil tohunga who had command over many atua. Pāwa lived at nearby Rangitoto (a range east of Te Kūiti) and had learned of Rona from one of his atua, who had reported that she was a kiritea, a fair-skinned young woman of charm, beauty and vivacity. After bathing with her friends one day, Rona was spirited away by invisible hands and conveyed to Pāwa's pā, where she was forced to become his wife.

When the distraught attendants brought news of her abduction in such an uncanny fashion, Rona's brother, Korokia, called on the suitors of his sister and their friends to rescue the young woman. The only person they knew who had the power to remove anyone in such a mysterious way was the dreaded Pāwa.

The young men assembled hastily and set out on their mission. They were fearful of Pāwa's powers and crept through the forest, avoiding the trails in the hope of rushing the pā and taking it by surprise. When they came to the edge of the forest they assembled in formation and ran swiftly across the open land, surrounding the pā. But their approach had been seen by keen eyes. Before they could reach the palisades a madness seemed to seize them. Many of them fell lifeless to the ground. Others turned on their friends and fierce fighting broke out among themselves. One hundred and fifty men had set out from the pā, but only one escaped. Korokia was the sole survivor of that gallant band of warriors.

The saddened remnant of the hapū discussed the matter at length and then sent a messenger to Hākawau, asking for his help. Hākawau was well known for his ability in warfare and when he heard that Rona had been abducted he was deeply grieved.

'If it were only a matter of leading a taua,' he said, 'I would gladly stand at their head, but this is a case of mākutu. Before such witchcraft I should be powerless and all that would happen would be that more brave men would die. Perhaps there is a solution. I will ask my father.'

Hākawau's father listened. 'Yes, there is a way that this evil person may be overcome. It will not be by taiaha and mere but by turning his own powers on him. Listen, my son, I have a brother who possesses the knowledge of mākutu and whose mana is greater than that of Pāwa. He lives in Te Urewera. You must make the long journey to him, my son, and tell him your story. By the womb that bore us both he will share with you the mystery of his art.'

Days and weeks passed. At length Hākawau returned to his father. 'To you, my father, and to my father's brother, I give thanks. I have learned the karakia that will overcome Pāwa's evil and the magic that will grind his face in the dust of the ground.'

Hākawau chose a small party of 50 men. There were 20 from Kāwhia and 30 from Waikato — the last of the toa of Korokia's hapū. They marched towards Rangitoto with no attempt at secrecy. Leaving his men in full sight of the enemy, Hākawau crept forward until he could see every detail of the pā. He saw Pāwa standing on a watchtower, gesticulating towards Korokia's warriors. With eyes that saw the invisible spirit world, Hākawau watched the atua of Pāwa converge on the unsuspecting men of Kāwhia and Waikato. Summoning all his strength and concentrating on the black knowledge he had learned from his uncle, Hākawau chanted the karakia that summoned the atua of Te Urewera.

To his trained gaze they materialised on the plain and began to attack Pāwa's atua. The place rang with the cries of the contending gods of war, with the thud of weapons, the hoarse panting of the fighters and the moans of the wounded. The atua of Te Urewera were experienced fighters.

Before long there was no sign of Pāwa's evil spirits.

Hākawau returned to his men. 'Let us go forward,' he said. 'The time of vengeance has come.'

One of his boldest warriors, whom none would accuse of timidity, stepped forward.

'Hākawau! I have followed you in many battles and I have borne myself as a warrior, but I tremble at your command. I can fight with flesh and blood, but the wairua will kill me before I could reach the outer palisades of the pā.'

'But the fight is over,' Hākawau said in surprise. 'I have been watching it and I have seen the atua of Pāwa defeated and dead. See for yourself.'

He led the way, his men following reluctantly. They had seen nothing of the fierce contest but they trusted Hākawau. He led them through the unmanned mazes of the palisades. Pāwa was no longer standing on the watchtower. He had seen the defeat of his atua and knew that his mana had been taken from him. He had gone inside his whare and waited for the end.

Hākawau sent for him and the chief was led up to him. Hākawau grasped his mere and advanced towards Pāwa. The mere trembled, advanced and retreated, and was brought close to Pāwa's head. But the blow did not fall. Hākawau brushed him lightly across the temple at the point where the skull is thin and a skilled man, with a sudden twist, can lift the top of a man's head. The mere left a thin trickle of blood where the edge had split the skin, without damaging the bone. He pulled the feathers from Pāwa's hair, dragged a greenstone pendant from his ear and threw his cloak on the ground.

'Your power has gone, Pāwa,' he said. 'Your karakia availed you little against mine. I will not kill you because I have shamed you. Remember in humility that your life was spared by Hākawau. You are no longer a tohunga, nor a rangatira. You are a tūtūā (person of no account).'

'And now, where is Rona?' he demanded abruptly.

The discredited tohunga meekly led his opponent to a whare and slid back the door. Rona came out. Her skin was still fair, her limbs were rounded, she was graceful in all her movements — and Hākawau found favour in her eyes. Sorrow was mingled with joy as she fell into his arms, and was taken back to her pā.

The Mauri of Pukekohe

The forests around Pukekohe were well stocked with kererū, tūī and kākā, which provided for the needs of the local people. The mauri stone was kept in a secret place on a hillside, the location of which was known to only a few people. The fame of the mauri and the abundance of birdlife that it ensured had spread as far as Te Urewera. A young rangatira of Tūhoe announced to his people that he was going to steal the mauri and bring it to them. It was an almost impossible task, for no one was likely to reveal such a closely guarded secret to him.

'You must be patient,' he told his people. 'I have a plan, but it will take more than one season to put it into effect.'

He left his home carrying fine garments and several treasured heirlooms, and travelled slowly across country until he came to the district of Pukekohe. He was made welcome at one of the larger kāinga where, because of his possessions and his noble appearance, he attracted the attention of a young woman of high lineage. He courted her and won her, and settled down as a member of his wife's tribe. He took part in all the activities of the kāinga and when the bird-hunting season came around it was natural for him to join the other young men on their expeditions into the forest.

He was pleasantly surprised to find how plentiful the birds were, how easy they were to catch and how fat and succulent they had become. He commented on this fact and was informed that the whole area was notable for birds because of the influence of the mauri. One of the guardians of the stone of fertility boasted to him that if one climbed the hill and held up his hands with the fingers spread far apart, the kererū would fly down and put their heads between the fingers.

The Tūhoe chief expressed polite incredulity saying that he could never believe such a thing unless he saw it for himself. His friend was nettled by the remark. A few days later he went up to him and said, 'If you do not believe me, I will take you myself. I can understand that you would not credit this thing because you are a stranger and come from Te Urewera where such things are not possible. Will you come with me now?'

The chief agreed and the two entered the forest. As they climbed up the hill the birds appeared on every tree. The guide stopped at a convenient spot and held up his hands. As he had said, the kererū flew down and put their heads between his fingers, which closed on their necks like a trap.

'Now will you believe?' he asked with a superior smile.

'I will believe because I have seen it for myself. But I think there must be some magic in your hands. It is your mana that has accomplished this amazing thing. This must be the true explanation; perhaps there is no mauri in this forest after all.'

The man was startled by the suggestion. 'Oh no, it is not my mana. The birds all come to Pukekohe because of the mauri.'

'No, I cannot believe that.'

'Very well, then. If you will swear not to reveal the secret, I will show you the sacred stone. It is well hidden but it lies not far from here.'

The young rangatira promised to keep the secret and was taken to a rātā tree. Hidden in a hollow below the trunk there was a stone. He looked at it appraisingly. It was not light, but it could be carried under one arm.

As the months passed he kept the knowledge of the mauri stone's location to himself. He continued to live in the village until it was time once more to fill the storehouses. He took little part in bird-hunting but joined the eeling parties, often staying out all night and not returning until late in the morning in order that the people would get used to his being away from home.

One evening he gathered up his greenstone ornaments and concealed them with some dried kūmara in the pocket of his belt. He set out alone on the pretence of catching eels. He made his way straight to the rātā tree, took out the sacred mauri, placed it in the basket he used for carrying eels and started his long journey home.

At daybreak the bird-spearers set out from the kāinga but when they entered the forest they were surprised by the quiet that seemed to have fallen on it. There was no sound of birds and no movement in the tree-tops. Wherever they went there was the same mysterious silence. With a dreadful sense of foreboding they went to the rātā and found that the mauri was missing. A kōrero was held on the marae and it was soon found that the rangatira of Tūhoe was also missing. Parties were sent to all the places where eels were caught, but there was no sign of him. They knew without doubt that he was the cunning thief who had stolen the sacred possession.

Two taua were soon on his trail, one travelling up the Waikato by canoe and the other marching overland. But the thief had a head start on them. After travelling by canoe up the river as far as Taupiri, he abandoned the canoe there and set off across country. He passed through the swamps and reached Maungatautari, but the stone grew heavier as he went and his pace slowed. He stopped where the trail led over a hill and looked back. His pursuers knew the way he was likely to take and he could see them not far behind.

Picking up the stone, he ran on, making for Rotorua. Now he could hear the shouts of the pursuring warriors. Before long they were so close that he could hear the sound of branches snapping off trees and the thud of many feet on the ground as they pursued him. In front of him was a lake. He knew there was no hope of eluding the pursuit or of taking the mauri to his own people, but after all his labours he was determined that no one but he should have possession of the stone. He threw himself over a bluff and, with the stone still clasped in his arms, sank swiftly down to the bottom of the lake.

Neither the rangatira of Te Urewera nor the mauri of Pukekohe were seen again. When the men of the taua returned sadly to their home, they found that there were few birds left in the forest. The sacred talisman had gone and could never be replaced. From that time onwards Pukekohe was no longer the happy hunting ground of the bird-spearers, but they say that the influence of the mauri, emanating from the waters of the lake, affected the forests round Rotorua and even extended to Te Urewera, where birds became more plentiful.

Te Hononga

Pīkari was working with his people at Tāmaki, digging trenches to assist the portage of canoes across the isthmus between the Manukau and Waitematā harbours. When they had finished he sent them off to their home at Kāwhia while he remained at Ōtāhuhu. An unknown force compelled him to continue his work. After some time he discovered the bones of a woman. He wrapped them in a mat intending to re-bury them. But, for some reason that he could not understand, he kept the bones in his whare and was constantly drawn to unwrap them and look at them. He realised that they were tapu and had been given into his keeping.

When his people returned they were intrigued by his habit of going frequently to the whare. They wondered what it could be that exercised such a fascination for their chief. However, Pīkari kept the door fastened and would not reveal his secret. The time came to transport the canoes over the narrow isthmus that separates the twin harbours and Pīkari divulged his secret to the old women who had accompanied the party. They took it as a sacred trust and wept over the bones. When the chief returned he said to the women, 'Keep watch. See that no one comes near while I bury the bones where they can never be found.'

The people all returned to Kāwhia and life in the pā settled down to its normal routine. But Pīkari was restless and unhappy. He longed to go back to Ōtāhuhu. The bones were calling to him. After trying in vain to resist the inexplicable urge, he took a small canoe and paddled up the coast and to the head of the Manukau Harbour. He made his way at once to the burial place and, as he reached it, he heard a voice say, 'Do not leave me again. Build a whare for yourself at this place and remain with me.'

With a curious sense of expectancy Pīkari built a tiny whare of raupō and thatched the roof roughly, waiting to see what would happen. Weeks went by and every day was the same. He made short expeditions to catch fish and eels and to snare birds. He accumulated a pile of food that he cooked and preserved in preparation for the winter.

One night he was lying on his mat in the whare wondering what power was keeping him so far away from his own people. He turned on his side, throwing out his arm restlessly, when he was astonished to find that his hand had come in to contact with living flesh. He moved it cautiously and felt the stomach and breast of a woman. A soft voice spoke.

'I am she whom you buried. I have come to life — for you.'

'Who are you?'

She placed her hand on his. 'You must not ask questions. Be content that I am here with you. All I can tell you is that I have come from another world. I cannot tell where I am from nor where I am going.'

'Will you remain with me forever, now that we have found each other?' Pīkari asked.

'No, my dear husband, that is not given to us. For one year I will be your wife and then I must leave you. By then a child will be given to us. I will go with you to your people and we will take the baby with us, but after that I must leave you.'

The time passed more quickly than Pīkari had ever known. In the daytime he hunted for food. At night his wife came to him and they lay in each other's arms until she left him before the dawn. When the time of labour came Pīkari gently assisted his wife and a baby girl was born to them. Together they launched the canoe, placed the baby in a bed of moss and soft feathers and travelled to the kāinga at Kāwhia. For the first time Pīkari saw his wife in the daylight and his heart was sad and rebellious at the thought that soon she would be leaving him.

The baby was left with Pīkari's people at Kāwhia to be tended and cared for, and husband and wife returned to their whare at Ōtāhuhu.

'I cannot bear to think of your leaving me,' he said. 'Stay with me, mother of my daughter.'

She smiled at him sadly. 'You must not think of the sorrow of parting, husband. Remember rather the joy of our year together and the new life we have created for our daughter. The year of happiness was a gift from the gods to you because you took my bones from the cold swamp and buried them and cared for them.'

'But will you not be grieved to leave me?'

'Yes, husband. Our year together has been the fulfilment of my life. There is only one thing I can leave you as a memento of our love. I will sing you love songs now that you will remember and that will become part of the heritage of your people.'

She rested her head on his bosom and sang sweetly to Pīkari. Tears flowed and wet his cheeks. He clung to her desperately trying to keep her with him, but with the songs still echoing in his ears she faded away and he was left alone.

Then began the time of agony and frustration of mind as Pīkari grieved for his wife. He was nearly demented. Nothing would induce him to leave his whare. His people came to him and begged him to return with them but he refused. He seldom hunted for food and became thin and weak. Often he would lie for hours, motionless, and at other times he would shake the framework of the house in a frenzy and bite his lips until the blood ran down his tattooed chin. He called his wife by name and sometimes the soft winds seemed to speak with her voice.

One night as he tossed restlessly from side to side on his sleeping mat, he had a vision of his wife. Her face was sad.

'Why are you grieving so for me, my beloved?'

'I cannot live without you.'

He stretched out his arms to her, but with infinite compassion in her eyes, she stepped back.

'Alas, my husband, you cannot touch me, for I belong to your world no longer. You have forgotten our happiness and have remembered only the sorrow. My spirit is always with you but our bodies cannot touch. I have come to tell you that I must always dwell in the spirit world. You must go to Kāwhia now to care for our daughter. Her name is Te Hononga (joined together), for she has been born to unite us forever.'

The spirit woman disappeared and through the night Pīkari thought of

147

her words. The next day some of his people arrived by canoe to urge him to return to them again and Pīkari allowed them to take him away.

As they drew near to the familiar headlands and beaches he felt a new strength surging in his veins. His thoughts were tumultuous but underneath there was a new strength and calmness. It was like the sea, tumbling in white-capped waves on the surface but calm and still and deep beneath, with thoughts of another world occasionally darting past, like fish whose silver bodies have caught a ray of sunlight.

There were many people waiting on the shore to greet him. Among them was a little girl who looked at him steadily. Her eyes held his, and the calm depths in his soul welled up strongly and silently like a floodtide, because her eyes were the eyes of the woman he loved.

GLOSSARY

ariki noble, great chief
aroha affection, love
atua gods, spirit
haere mai! welcome!
haka dance
hapū sub-tribe, clan
haumia fern root
huata spear
huia bird with distinctive tail feathers
iwi tribe
kāhu hawk
kāinga unfortified village
kākā parrot
kākahu kura red-feathered cloak
kao dried kūmara
karakia chant, incantation
kauati stick for fire-making
kawau shag
kererū wood pigeon
kiore rat
kiwi flightless bird
kō digging implement
kōkōwai red ochre mixed with shark oil

kono basket
kōrari flax stalk
kōrero talk, speech, discussion
kōtuku white heron
kūmara sweet potato
kura red; treasured object
maero ferocious forest creatures
māipi shark-tooth knife
mākutu black magic
mana integrity, influence, prestige
mānuka tea tree
manuhiri guest, visitor
marae plaza, courtyard
maro loincloth
mauri life-force, talisman
mere greenstone club
moa large extinct bird
mōkihi raft
moko tattoo
muka dressed flax
ngārara lizard, monster
ngerengere leper
ope large group, war party
pā fortified village

parawai   superior cloak
patupaiarehe   fairy-like
  creatures
pāua   abalone shellfish
ponaturi   sea fairy
pounamu   greenstone
pouwhenua   weapon
puhi   high-born young woman
pūtōrino   flute
rangatira   chief, noble
Rarohenga   underworld, spirit
  world
raupō   reed, bulrush
rimurapa   seaweed
rua   storage pit
taiaha   staff-like weapon
tamariki   children
tāne   husband, man
taniwha   monster
tangi   ceremonial mourning
tapu   sacred, forbidden
tapuwae   footstep, footprint
taua   war party
tāwhiti   trap
Te Ao Mārama   world of light,
  ,everyday world
tēnā koe   hello

Te Rēinga   leaping place of
  spirits
tī kōuka   cabbage tree
tiki   neck ornament
tipua   enchanted; demon,
  guardian spirit
tohunga   expert, priest
tūhua   obsidian
tūī   parson bird
tuna   eel
tūtūā   commoner
umu   earth oven
wahine   woman
waiata   song
wairua   soul, spirit
waka   canoe
waka taua   war canoe
weka   wood hen
wharau   hut, shelter
whare   house
wharekura   school of
  instruction
wharepuni   sleeping house
whare tapere   house of
  entertainment
whata   food storage platform